TOWARD YOU

PROPERTY OF

TOWARD YOU

Jim Krusoe

Tin House Books
Portland, Oregon & New York, New York

Copyright © 2011 Jim Krusoe

All rights reserved. No part of this book may be used or reproduced in
any manner whatsoever without written permission from the publisher
except in the case of brief quotations embodied in critical articles or
reviews. For information, contact Tin House Books, 2617 NW Thurman
St., Portland, OR 97210.

Published by Tin House Books, Portland, Oregon, and New York,
New York
Distributed to the trade by Publishers Group West, 1700 Fourth St.,
Berkeley, CA 94710, www.pgw.com

Library of Congress Cataloging-in-Publication Data

Krusoe, James.
 Toward you / Jim Krusoe. -- 1st U.S. ed.
   p. cm.
 ISBN 978-0-9825691-1-5
 I. Title.
 PS3561.R873T76 2011
 813'.54--dc22

                      2010045863

First U.S. edition 2011
Printed in Canada
Interior design by Janet Parker
www.tinhouse.com

ELKINS PARK FREE LIBRARY
563 CHURCH ROAD
ELKINS PARK, PA 19027-2445

Somewhere someone is traveling furiously toward you,
At incredible speed, traveling day and night,
Through blizzards and desert heat, across torrents,
    through narrow passes.
But will he know where to find you,
Recognize you when he sees you,
Give you the thing he has for you?

—JOHN ASHBERY, from "At North Farm"

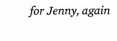

for Jenny, again

1

Testing. One. Two.

2

I'd been tinkering with the Communicator when I heard a short squeal of brakes outside my house and then a dull thud: the sound of a body being struck by a speeding car. As quickly as I could I removed the headset, shut off the current, and hurried to my front door. When I opened it, I looked around.

The street was pretty much empty except for a big brown dog wobbling up the walk to where I stood. About five feet away, it suddenly sat down and stared as if it knew me but was having trouble remembering from where exactly, and whether I'd been a friend or an enemy. The dog's dark eyes moved from deep, pained questioning, to blank, then back to me.

"Hey, boy," I said, but before the animal could come to any resolution one way or another, it fell heavily onto its side, all four legs stuck out and quivering. I tried to remember if I'd seen it around the neighborhood and, if so, where, but in truth I'd never paid much attention to dogs. The animal looked at me again, let out a sort of exasperated sigh, as if it had done what it was supposed to do—had brought back the ball, or whatever, and dropped it at my feet. "And now," it seemed to say, "it's your turn." But my turn to do *what*, I couldn't understand.

Then it died.

The dog, a male, had short red-brown hair with a small patch of white on its chest and a flat, broad skull. His expression, in death, had changed to one of dignity and regret. I walked over and patted his stony head. "Sorry, guy," I told him. "You did OK. You came to the right house. It wasn't your fault. You did fine. It just didn't happen to work out. Things go that way sometimes. Believe me, I should know."

Around the dog's neck was a thick leather collar with silver spikes and an oval nameplate with *Bob* in block letters, but there was no other identification—no license, no rabies tag, no carefully chosen heart-shaped or bone-shaped or round disk with an address to look up or a phone number to call—nobody at all to tell the bad news.

And as chance would have it, Bob was my name, too.

Bob's nails were dark, shiny, and in need of cutting. There was an endearing tuft of black hair at the very tip of his tail. His tongue, already drained to gray in the fading light, poured carelessly out from one side of his loose mouth. I could see no visible marks on him, but clearly he had been the victim of that speeding car—wherever it had disappeared to—the sound of whose driver's belated attempt to brake had disturbed me. It seemed odd that out of all the doors on this street Bob might have staggered toward, he had chosen one that belonged to a person who shared his name—his brother, in effect—but animals, I knew, often had a way of sensing the nearness of a kindred spirit.

Or, alternately, I thought, if Bob *hadn't* known my name, was it possible he'd been sent as a sign? Could Bob's visit be a warning, like in that famous scene in *The Godfather* when the horse's head is left on the movie producer's bed? Was someone or some thing telling me: "Hey pal, it's time to wake up. Bob was alive. Now he is dead. You are alive, but how long do you think that is going to last? So carpe diem, Bob, if you get my drift"?

I may have been missing a couple of steps in the old reasoning process here, but the point was the same. In other words, there was a possibility, however remote, that some godlike force had chosen this unfortunate dog to send me a message, and that message was: "Get off your ass, Bob. It's time to stop your woolgathering and to make something of your life. You've been working on the Communicator in a more or less half-assed fashion ever since Yvonne disappeared, and how far have you gotten? Not very, is how far. You've been putting on those headphones and taking them off for how long? Since Yvonne's been gone, that's how long. Don't let me lose more faith in you than I have already, but also, don't spend so much time on your invention that you forget you have an upholstery business to maintain. I could tell you dozens of stories of people who starved to death before they finally found what they were looking for. Still, as it did for this unfortunate animal, the messenger of this message, time is running out for you, too. That ship, or train, or bus supposed to take you out of here to a better future is at the station and is about to move on without you unless you get onboard."

As messages went, I thought it could have been a little more focused. *The messenger of this message*? And *woolgathering*? Where did that come from? I'd never used that word in my whole life. Why was I using it now?

I took a few steps down the walk, toward the street, and turned to look at my house. It was a modest frame structure with a mostly brown front yard and some kind of bush on the right side of the door. True, the door could have used another coat of varnish and the bush's leaves were starting to curl, but we were in a water shortage. That wasn't the whole story, however. The fact was that I had neglected to do the watering as well—yet another strike against me, the dog's message might have added, in a sort of *PS*. To make matters worse, my gutters were stuffed with leaves. My next-door neighbor, Farley, had a tree whose branches hung over my roof, and though I'd asked him a million times to cut it back, he refused. One of these days I was going to have to get a ladder to clean those gutters out. I hated heights.

I knew I should call the city and report Bob's death, but the truth was that the dog's timing was terrible. It was five-thirty on a Thursday, and the city offices were already closed for the day. As a cost-cutting move, they were closed on Fridays, so no one would be answering phones again until the following Monday—no, Tuesday, because Monday was Columbus Day. In other words, when—about five days in the future—I finally got through to the city switchboard and sat on hold for about ten minutes listening to an idiotically cheerful trumpet solo that some well-meaning civil servant must believe represents the sound of a happy citizenry, was connected to a clerk, and had to explain how the previous week an animal had died on my doorstep, how long would it be from then before someone actually appeared to take said animal away? Over a month ago I'd called to ask them to take away a metal bookshelf that had been tossed near the curb in front of my house, and large parts of it still remained, making a clanking sound every time a car ran over one of them. So I figured that from where I was right now, time-wise, to the actual moment a bored maintenance worker arrived at my small house to carry Bob away, I would have a dead dog lying across my threshold for a minimum of five days, with a week far more likely, possibly two.

Also, there would be the smell.

It didn't seem right, somehow. Bob had done his job. Bob had made his painful way all that distance, up my walk nearly to my front door, and had, like the inventor of the marathon, Philippides, used his last precious moments of life to deliver his message. That, and maybe to beg for a little first aid. And I *had* gotten the message, more or less, but, pitifully, had been unable to offer any assistance in the area of veterinary expertise. Surely Bob deserved more than being thrown into a landfill, or worse.

When I considered it, I had only two real options. The first was to drag Bob next door into Farley's yard and let Farley deal with him. The downside of that was if Farley happened to be around at this hour and he saw me (Farley worked nights, and his schedule seemed to change often, so I could never be sure exactly when he was at home), I would be in big trouble. Farley had a nasty sense of boundary entitlement and once, when a letter addressed to me had been delivered to his house by mistake, he wouldn't hand it over until I signed for it. It turned out to be an overdue notice from the library. Or I could just drag Bob back out to the street and leave him, but the negative in that case was that if anyone saw me doing it—and there was a lot of potential to be seen because half my neighborhood, come to think of it, was out of work—I might be accused of murder, or at least littering. Plus, lying in the road, Bob could cause an accident; the last thing I wanted was to hurt an innocent mom driving her kid to preschool and then be sued by her hotshot lawyer.

I walked back to where Bob was lying and thought it over: Why *not* be active for a change? What was it Bob had said about woolgathering? When all was said and done, it would be a simple enough thing to drag Bob around back and bury him beneath the rosebush that was currently looking in serious need of nutrition. All in all, I guessed it wouldn't take more than a half hour, and, in addition, it would give the brave dog a sort of resting place in honor of his sacrifice. For another thing, it would feed the bush.

The more I pondered, the better the idea seemed. I looked down at the inert form lying at my feet. "You were wondering if I was a friend or foe, Bob," I told the ex-man's-best-friend, "but you can relax now. You made the right choice. You did the right thing. You're safe now. Nobody is ever going to scold you again for jumping up on the furniture, for tracking mud onto the carpet, or for stealing an unguarded pork roast from a dining room table while your underachiever owner is a room away in his La-Z-Boy recliner—a real pain to reupholster, by the way. You're a good dog, Bob, and notice that while only a few minutes ago you were accusing me of being indecisive, look at me now. I'm taking action on your behalf, my friend. And that's only the beginning."

Grabbing Bob by his hind legs, I pulled him around the side of my house through the gate to the backyard and left him about four feet away from the rosebush. He looked as if he were sleeping, though his original look of regret had turned to one of resentment. Then I went to the garage and found the fancy spade I'd bought from a mail-order gardening catalog but had put off using because it looked so beautiful. I took it down and started to dig. My backyard was small, so at first the hole seemed disproportionately large, but once I'd slid Bob inside, the hole suddenly looked too small and too shallow. I could have pulled him out again and dug it deeper, but decided not to.

"Rest in peace, old buddy," I whispered.

There might be a little smell, but eventually the odor would disappear. It wouldn't be the worst smell in the neighborhood, either, that honor probably going to Farley's taxidermy shed. In time, Bob would become the rosebush and the rosebush would become Bob. Or something like that. It was a nice thought, I thought.

I filled the hole and tamped it down. Then I watered the rosebush for several minutes. The backyard looked worse, in its way, than the front, but at least back there people weren't leaving me notes to pick up my trash or to cut my grass. In the darkening air I could just barely make out a hawthorn at the far corner of the yard that was in the process of shriveling to a Brillo pad. The lemon tree, I noticed, was covered with cobwebs, which meant the white flies were back. I shut off the water and hung the spade back up in the garage, where I found a piece of wood—a sawed-off end of a one-by-twelve I'd used to make a shelf a while ago. Then I unearthed a brush and some paint. In a kind of Old English lettering, I wrote, *Bob*, and beneath it I added the date and the letters *RIP*. I carried the finished sign over to the rosebush and hammered it into the ground about a foot away from where Bob's head ought to be. All in all, it looked pretty professional.

That night, I dreamed I was walking up and down the streets of St. Nils, some of which I recognized and some I didn't, when I found myself in an unfamiliar alley, staring at a large building that appeared to be a warehouse, strangely out of place amid all the nearby homes. How the warehouse had come to be among all these residential structures, and why such an anomalous eyesore was tolerated, I had no way of knowing. The building was about thirty feet high, and the side I faced was about sixty feet long. There were two windows on top and two on the bottom, each about twelve feet by six feet, and no entrance was visible. Flat iron bars covered the lower set of windows, dividing them into checkerboards. The upper row of windows had no bars at all, only closed gray shutters with flaking paint.

Peculiarly, between the building's top story and the lower one, someone had painted a squiggly horizontal line, with everything below the line a light blue, while the top section, except for the shutters, was completely white. This contrast, along with the fact that the line was vaguely wavelike, gave the place the feeling of an ocean on its lower part, and of a cloud-filled sky on its upper one. Except for the oversized copper gutters along its flat roof, there was little else in the way of decoration, nor was there any company name or logo printed anywhere to signal who owned it. I couldn't be sure if the building was still occupied or had been abandoned and was only waiting to be torn down. Or possibly rehabbed into low-priced artists' lofts. Artists, I remembered thinking in my dream, will live about anywhere.

I knew, of course, that if I walked around to another side of the building I might find some clue to tell me more, but as it was a dream, it was impossible to move from where I was rooted. Why had I come there in the first place? Or, alternatively, was there some message *I* was supposed to deliver to whoever was inside, and, if so, where would I find the front door?

Then I woke. I got out of bed and walked into my living room, where I looked out the front window.

Across the street a light went on. A man wearing pajamas and a robe appeared at his window and looked back at me. Had his dreams been strange, too? Was he lonely? Did he want to step into the street to have a late-night chat?

Thus, I wondered, and then I wondered if he was wondering the same things. After a few minutes his light went out, and his window was dark again. A street or so away, a car backfired. It was well after midnight, so I washed my hands, brushed my teeth again, and this time finally stayed asleep.

3

Testing, testing, one, two, three, four. Testing—is anybody out there?

Testing. Anybody? Testing.

Can you hear me?

And, of course, there's nothing here, let alone a microphone.

4

I first came up with the idea of the Communicator back in the days when I was still a student at the Institute for Mind/Body Research. I was in my twenties then—just a kid, really—and after flunking out of St. Nils Community College thanks to a faculty more concerned with applying artificial standards to measure knowledge than with making it possible for a person to receive a real education, I found out about the institute in our local alternative paper.

Let me say it frankly: I had not been a huge success in high school, either academically or socially. But mostly I had succeeded in pushing many of the details of my physical appearance out of my mind until one evening when my high school classmates and I were sitting around the end-of-term bonfire, making a game out of deciding what animals people looked like. Someone, a girl actually, chose to describe me as "a perfect capybara," which—none of us but her ever having seen one—left me undisturbed until the following morning when I looked it up in the single volume of the *World Book Encyclopedia* I owned, unfortunately the *C*. The capybara, I discovered, is the world's largest rodent, roughly the weight of an average human, and more than anything resembles a guinea pig with slightly longer legs. It is a favorite food of the anaconda, the world's largest snake. Also, it tastes like pork, and its skin can be stretched only in one direction, which makes it a favorite of glove makers all over the world. There were places, I learned, where various state and municipal governments gave a bounty for killing them. I took a good look in the mirror. The girl had been right. What woman would ever want to date a capybara? But the bright side of that experience was that the research I did that morning began a lifelong interest in animals—not a bad thing for someone who spends most of his time alone.

It was during my very first visit to the Institute for Mind/Body Research that its brilliant and charismatic founder, Howard Bonano, explained to me that his mission "was to improve mankind's knowledge of two outstanding areas of human experience: the mind and the body." An intense-looking, slightly overweight individual of medium height, Howard Bonano had a shock of dark black hair, except for one white lock that erupted straight above his left eye and swept back over his skull like a plastic grocery bag pasted by the wind to the fender of a speeding car. He wore thick glasses with heavy, black plastic frames, and even before I settled in as a student there, he had sized me up.

"You," he had said, pointing toward the Mind Building, "forget your body. You belong on that side." Then he led me straight to the financial aid office, where he arranged to subsidize my first year of study through a hefty student loan.

A semester later, after I had made a strong showing in Auraology and Past Life Regressology (at one point, I had apparently been swallowed by an anaconda), I walked into Howard Bonano's class in channeling the dead. It was there that I first began to formulate the principles for what one day would be the Communicator, even though my actual methodology turned out to be far different than the techniques outlined in Bonano's syllabus.

My idea for the Communicator—although it wasn't named back then—was the result of two distinct circumstances. First, while most of my fellow students seemed to have no trouble at all calling up, more or less at will, various deceased individuals—mostly famous people or celebrities—I could not, as Howard Bonano once announced in front of the entire class, "raise a rat in a garbage dump."

The second circumstance, which I mentioned earlier, was Yvonne.

Throughout the first several weeks of school I had stayed mainly on the mind side of campus, trying halfheartedly to meet various girls and then watching them walk away. I didn't blame them. Still, I had gotten into the habit of attending the biweekly vegetarian mixers held in the institute's parking lot, not so much to mix as for the food, which was quite good, and it was at one of these affairs that I met Yvonne, who was wearing black shorts and a red tank top made of stretchy material and standing off to one side of a group of her body-oriented friends, looking comparatively thoughtful. I approached her, and to my question of what she was doing at the institute, she replied that she was studying various types of movement and several kinds of massage. She mentioned that she had begun to write a little poetry, though she still considered herself an amateur. Her legs were light tan and long.

"That's great," I remember saying. "You can't go wrong with poetry."

"Yes," she said, "that's what I think, too, but still I get kidded about it by some of these more body-centered types." (She pointed to a fit-looking guy wearing a sleeveless tee shirt and a sweatband. He waved back and blew her a kiss.) "They claim it smacks a little too heavily of mind, but I don't agree, and I must say it means a lot to me to find another person who's able to recognize the finer things in life. Thank you." She seemed genuinely appreciative of my remark, and more importantly, she wasn't walking away.

I looked at Yvonne's own body, which was glowing in the warmth of the evening, forming moist, inviting circles beneath the armpits of her tank top. She lifted her arm to remove a leaf or something from her hair, and I could see she must have just shaved that morning; her skin there was especially tender looking.

"And you, Bob, what are you studying?" she asked.

I shut my eyes. "Um," I said. "Right now I'm pretty much struggling to communicate with the dead."

"Then I guess," she said, "you're one of those channel people. I've heard some amazing stories; that must be so interesting."

"Oh, those," I answered. "They're good enough as far as they go, I suppose, although I'm working on another method entirely." Not that I *had* been, of course, but I needed to say something fast to keep me from sounding like a complete loser.

"Really," she said. "Do you suppose you could explain?"

"It's less complicated than you might think," I said. Meanwhile I prayed that an idea would occur to me.

I took a breath and tried to remember what Howard Bonano had told us on the first day of class. Something about how the dead were really, really anxious to talk with us, because they missed everything about the earth so much, especially (for some reason) keeping up with the new movies and TV shows, in which department we could be most helpful. Certainly, this seemed to be confirmed by the conversations my fellow students had reported.

Yvonne nodded. "Go on."

"OK," I continued, "well, obviously, the dead can't talk like you and I are talking at this moment . . ." I thought for a second . . . "because they don't have vocal cords."

I had Yvonne's attention.

"So," I filled in the gap, and at that exact moment, I began to formulate the rudimentary principles of what would later be called the Communicator: "OK . . . well . . . in the first place, these dead people clearly must use some other form of sound waves, waves that I call . . ." (and what *would* I call them, I wondered) " . . . uh . . . Terminal Waves, which although I don't yet understand how exactly the dead can produce them, once I actually make a connection, it will be simple enough to just ask them and find out. And in the second place . . . that's all I'm authorized to say at this time." I liked that word, *authorized*.

"But if this is true," Yvonne asked, "and these Terminal Waves are all around us, why don't we hear them all the time?"

"A good question," I answered. "That's exactly what I'm trying to find out, and believe me, once I do, then everyone will be able to hear them, and not just those people who tell us they're channeling and to trust them."

"You know," Yvonne said, "you're sort of funny looking, but I like you and I can tell you're really smart."

In the days and weeks to come, I kept asking myself if I was awake or in some prolonged and fantastic dream. Yvonne was beautiful, with glossy black hair, glowing skin, and straight eyebrows. I lost count of the nights that the two of us would be the last to leave the student lounge, her reading her poetry to me and combing my hair, and me touching various parts of her body above and beneath her clothing. "You have such wonderful brown hair," she used to say. "It's so rich and supple. It's like—I don't know—some animal's."

I had never been so happy. In addition, Howard Bonano agreed to let me drop the channeling course. One afternoon when Yvonne and I stopped by his office, he suggested that I just reenroll in a couple of semesters, pay for it all over again, and give it another try. "You never know, Bob,"

Howard Bonano said. "Things that are really important often take a lot more time than you might guess." He gave Yvonne a wink.

Then, without warning, one Monday soon after that, I was on my way to a special seminar called "Speed-reading with the Third Eye," when Yvonne stopped me outside the classroom.

"Bob," she said, "if you have a minute, I think we need to talk."

I looked inside the room. Some of the students were sitting at their desks with their blindfolds already in place; others were whispering quietly. Turning back to Yvonne, I noticed she had what appeared to be a massive hickey on the left side of her neck. Also, she seemed more somber than usual, and somehow wiser as well, though I couldn't say what gave me that impression.

"Yvonne," I said, "has anything happened? Are you all right? Are you having some problem with your poetry? Is your body OK?"

Yvonne fixed me with the sort of look a person might give a distant relation who has shown up at her front door with three suitcases and a cat carrier. "As a matter of fact, Bob," she said, firmly but not unkindly, "I'll make this snappy. First, I want you to know you've been a real help with my poetry, and second that I've enjoyed knowing you. You're not a horrible person, Bob—far from it—only it just so happens that the other night I encountered—not for the first time, exactly, but in a way that I could get to appreciate the extent of his true genius—one of the master communicators of the universe, in mind and—tough luck for you, Bob—in body also, in which area I have to say you could use a little work, though in the past I was giving you the benefit of the doubt in favor of all the stuff I believed you were doing with your mind, even though not much has come of it so far.

"Look, Bob, I don't want to spoil this seminar, which I'm sure will be a good one for you," she said, "but I came by this morning to tell you that I can't go on living a lie. As of this very minute, I plan never to see you again, unless our paths cross by chance, of course. I'm in love, Bob, and this is my good-bye. Good luck. Don't give up on women. I'm sure one day you'll find someone who can see your good qualities in the same way as I have." She gave me a small kiss on the cheek. Her shiny black hair was held in place by a light yellow ribbon running across the top of her head, and she wore a white and yellow dress that came to her knees. It looked as if she had tried to slap a little face powder on the hickey, but it hadn't helped much.

"In love ..." I said out loud, but I thought, "With whom?" as meanwhile Yvonne walked away, not even looking back.

I never made it to that seminar. Instead, I staggered back to my dorm room with its plaid bedspread, beige paint, linoleum floor, and a poster of The Jackson Five on the wall closest to the bathroom. On the wall above my bed was a poster of recently excavated Roman roads. It showed a field with yellow wildflowers, a ragged line of bricks running right through them, beneath a bright blue sky. Yvonne had found it at a garage sale and bought it as a present for me. "Every time you look at it you can think of me," she said, and she'd been right.

I stared at both the posters. Michael Jackson was gone, killed by drugs, and Marlon Jackson was into real estate. The roads were gone, mostly covered by dirt and buildings and sheep, even though in the poster, parts of them had returned, unearthed, like a hickey where the makeup covering it has washed off. Now Yvonne was gone, too.

The next day I packed my bags and left the Institute for Mind/Body Research forever. In order to pay back my considerable student loan, I became an apprentice to an upholsterer, and I eventually opened my own business, which I named Bob's Upholstery.

But all that—as they say—is history.

5

Come on, somebody—please hear me. How long do you think I can stay here doing this?

Don't answer that.

6

The morning after I buried Bob was a Friday, and I was just removing the seat of an antique chair on which the red leather had been clawed—the work of a cat, most likely—when I heard a knock at my front door. It was a sound so tentative and discreet that if I hadn't been pausing at that very moment to search for a pair of chisel-pliers, I probably would have missed it entirely. I opened the door to see a woman and a young girl, both with dark hair in pigtails that were parted so tightly I could see the pink lines of their scalps, a capital *I* and a lower case *i*, without the dot. The woman was wearing a dress made of deerskin and matching moccasins, and she had a beaded band across her forehead. Poking up from behind her head were two feathers that I thought were goose. The girl, who appeared to be her daughter, was dressed like a regular kid in a red jumper and silver tennis shoes. She looked as if she didn't want to be there. The chief difference between them, other than their age and the fact that while the mom had a touch of the reticent bunny about her, her daughter went more toward the cat family—in addition to the fact that the mom was wearing Native American clothing, of course—was that the daughter's arm was wrapped in fresh gauze, and the mother's was not. I looked closely at the woman. I opened my mouth and closed it. I tried again, and nothing happened.

Finally, I said, "Yvonne," because that's exactly who it was.

"Bob," she replied, "is that you?"

"It is," I said. "And what is with that outfit you are wearing? Have you become a Native American, or were you always one and I just didn't know it?" It was a stupid thing to ask, but I had to start somewhere.

Yvonne pulled the sides of her mouth into an embarrassed grimace, obviously struggling with her emotions. Then she bravely launched forward. "I'm sorry to be troubling you again after all these years, Bob." She paused to adjust one of the shoulders of her dress, and I noticed her neck was smooth and even. "I hadn't expected that when I knocked on this door I would find you behind it, and it's a big surprise, to say the very least. This is my daughter, Dee Dee. We're sorry to barge in on you like this, but yesterday, Dee Dee was waiting out in front of our duplex while I ran back inside to get her lunch for school, which I'd left on the kitchen counter, and a strange dog walked up and bit her."

She pointed to the Dee Dee's arm and the girl stuck out her tongue at me. "Naturally, I took her to the emergency room, where eventually they got round to bandaging her. The nurse said she'll be fine, but she also suggested it might not be a bad idea to see if we could track down the animal that did it. I should have started yesterday, but the whole morning was pretty much taken up with hanging out in emergency, and then I had to go to work that afternoon, so things got away from me, but today I have some time to spare before I have to go back to the casino—this is my uniform, to answer your question—so I thought I'd spend an hour or two at least trying to follow the nurse's advice. There's no real harm done to Dee Dee, as you can see, thank goodness, but you don't happen to know anyone who owns a fair-sized brown dog, do you? I'd hate to hear about some other child being bitten and not have tried to stop it. The fact is, I've been knocking on a lot of doors this morning, and I came to yours completely by chance. I hope that, after all these years, you're not still angry."

I looked down at Dee Dee, who had begun to rock slightly from side to side, evidently bored by this whole witch hunt. On the tape holding the gauze in place, someone had pasted a sticker of one of those circles with an insipid smile inside. Had anyone ever done a history of that hideous symbol? I wondered. How far back did it go? Surely it must have had an inventor, because I didn't remember seeing it at all when I was a child, then—bingo!—it was everywhere. And now that it had taken hold, would it eventually disappear over time, or was the human race doomed to carry it, like a mutated gene, through all eternity? Beneath the smiley face someone had added a set of crossbones to make it into a kind of pirate flag. Dee Dee stopped rocking and then crossed and uncrossed her eyes.

"Angry?" I said. "Me?"

Yvonne gave a small shrug. "So you wouldn't have any idea of who the dog's owner is, would you, Bob?" She paused, I supposed, on the off chance that she would hear a bark from inside my house, or maybe that the culprit himself would come bounding up behind me with a snarl. "We just moved back into the area, so I don't know many people except for those at the casino. Actually, we live a few blocks away, but everyone on our street is away at work, so I had to expand my search a lot farther than I'd planned. I have to say it's amazing to see you again after all these years."

"Let me think about it for a minute," I said, and I did. The years between her studies at the body section of the institute and that morning had been kind to Yvonne, and suddenly it seemed that no time at all had passed since I'd watched her walk away from me without a backward look. What had her life been like in between then and now? Surely, she couldn't be too happy to have to dress up in that silly costume for work every day, but there had to be more (well, there *was* Dee Dee, that was true). I had never thought Yvonne was the vengeful type, but could it be that by tracking down the owner of the dog she was fishing for a nice cash settlement? It was possible. There was something—I couldn't say what—that made me certain she was a single mom and could probably use some extra cash for buying her daughter shoes and whatnot.

The first dog that came to mind, naturally, was Bob, but I said nothing for the obvious reason that I didn't know who Bob's owner was, so there was no person I could have sent Yvonne to interview. Also, the more I thought about it, I could not ignore the unfavorable circumstances of Yvonne's former farewell. She had to know how much she had hurt me then, and for me to stand here now and simply offer up a chunk of useless information gratis would only confirm in her mind that I was the kind of guy she remembered—the kind she could treat badly and who would still come back for more, in other words: a needy, giant guinea pig. In my experience, that phrase "getting even" contained a world of wisdom, for unless two people met as equals, how could they ever hope to build, or rebuild, a real relationship?

More importantly though, if Bob *had* been the biter—and really, there must be about a million fair-sized brown dogs out there—hadn't he been punished enough? If Bob had bitten, well, he had bitten, and then, through some seldom-applied principle of cosmic retribution, he had been killed for it. Period. Whoever said, "De mortuis nil nisi bonum," had a point. I'd written that *RIP* on Bob's memorial, and now, less than twenty-four hours later, here was someone who had once carelessly broken my heart asking me to break my promise to Bob. I tried to think of some other dog I'd seen lurking in the neighborhood that I could recommend to Yvonne but couldn't. Dee Dee put one foot on top of the other and stood there, balancing. Clearly, this expedition was not the child's idea.

So would it help to tell Yvonne, "Well, I don't know who the owner might have been, but if you need a scapegoat

I just happen to have one in my backyard that you could exhume if that would make you feel better and, in the process, expose this innocent child to the edifying spectacle of a decaying animal"? I doubted it. Talk about trying to do anything to please!

Likewise, would it have been fair to condemn Bob without a fair trial? Then this attractive former girlfriend of mine and her daughter would return home, happily misinformed in the belief that the culprit had been punished (and how!) and completely give up searching for the real culprit who, the odds were, was still out there, chewing his way through a whole lineup of other little girls clutching their stuffed ponies and Hello Kitties. And then, there was one last consideration: if there was any chance at all that the flame that once flickered between us could be reignited, would the two of us standing together over a rotting dog corpse be the best way to do it? I was no expert in the ways of women, but I was guessing it would not.

Oh yes, plus one more thing: suppose it *could* somehow be shown beyond a doubt that Bob *had* been the biter—then how was I to prove Bob wasn't my dog? He had my name, for one thing, and for another, he was buried in my own backyard. I supposed I could ask Farley to appear in court, but given the perfidious nature of the man's character, I had no reason to believe he'd tell the truth.

"I'm really sorry," I told Yvonne. "I wish I could be more helpful, but I can't. On the other hand, if you and Dee Dee would like to take a little break from your hunt—I don't mean to pressure you, but Dee Dee's looking a little peaked, if you ask me—it so happens that I have a yellow cake I baked a couple of days ago and haven't had a chance to try out. I'd love for you both to come inside and have a piece. Do you suppose Dee Dee would be willing to help me test my cake, and maybe while she's eating the two of us can catch up on what's happened since we last saw each other?"

Dee Dee's eyes got large at the mention of cake, and she tugged at her mother's arm. "Well . . ." Yvonne hesitated, rightly wary of walking back into the emotion-packed world of the past. Still, she appeared tired herself, and she obviously wanted to please Dee Dee. "We *have* had a stressful morning. If it's not too much trouble, Bob, we'd love to test a piece of your yellow cake—wouldn't we, Dee Dee?"

Dee Dee looked up at me and nodded hard several times. She was a cute kid, no doubt, when she wasn't bored out of her mind. I ushered them inside, and along the way I noticed that one of Yvonne's moccasins was soaking wet. She must have stepped in a puddle, and it gave her a particular vulnerable quality. "Have a seat," I said, pointing at the leather couch a customer had left to be repaired about five years ago. Its legs were made of six real deer hooves. "I'll go into the kitchen to serve the cake. You relax; there are some magazines on the coffee table you may enjoy looking through. Oh, and, by the way, I couldn't help but see that your left shoe must be uncomfortable, being wet and all. Would you like to take it off and I can pop it in the toaster oven at really low heat? I'd guess that, given the fact it appears to be deerskin, like your dress, it won't take more than ten or fifteen minutes to dry as good as new. If you want me to, I can rub a little neatsfoot oil on it to keep it soft."

"That won't be necessary, Bob," Yvonne said, but she seemed to brighten at my offer. "Though, if you don't mind me saying so, you seem to know an awful lot about leather for such a mentally oriented person."

"Oh," I said, "I didn't mean to offend you. These days I re-cover furniture for a living, and I do most of my work right here. The couch you're sitting on is an example of what I do, and I particularly like to work with leather. In a way, it's like living in a room full of large pets, but ones you don't have to feed and which don't move around all the time. You probably don't know it, but I dropped out of the institute shortly after we spoke that last time, and so I suppose I owe you this career. Whatever happened to you at the institute? Were you ever able to graduate? Do you still write poetry?"

"Well," Yvonne said, and her expression grew somber, "that's a long story, and the fact is I dropped out of the institute soon after you did because I was pregnant with Dee Dee. I guess that institute was tough on both of us, in a way." She paused, as if in thought, and then resumed. "I like leather too, although the way we obtain it seems unnecessarily cruel, don't you agree?"

I nodded, and Yvonne bit her lip. "And yes, as a matter of fact, I still write poetry. Currently, I'm working on a series of interlinked haiku about my job as a waitress at the Chumash Village Indian Casino, in which I describe my fellow employees and many of our regulars—mostly hopeless gamblers and alcoholics—along with some of their favorite foods. The few people I've read them to seem to like them." She looked around the room, and her gaze settled on the pile of equipment on my workbench covered by a blue tarp. "My, that looks interesting. What's that?"

"I don't know if you remember that course I took back at the institute with Howard Bonano," I said, and Yvonne made a little face, "but I'm still trying to figure out a way to make some kind of a bridge between the living and the dead. I guess you could call it a hobby of mine. I call my device the Communicator, but I can't say I've made a lot of progress."

Dee Dee stuck her hands into the cracks between the couch cushions, fishing around for loose change. One of these days she was going to need braces, and I wondered if Yvonne could afford them.

Yvonne watched me watching her daughter. "Yes, I guess you could say that a lot of things turn out to be disappointing as we grow older, don't they?" Then she brightened. "I think that Dee Dee's getting restless. I don't want to be rude, but did you say something about a piece of cake?"

I went into the kitchen to prepare three plates. When I returned, Dee Dee was clicking the top of a ballpoint pen she must have found between the cushions. "The thing I like about furniture," Yvonne said, as she and Dee Dee ate their cake, "is it's always so straightforward. You can trust it; a piece of furniture will wait for you to use it when you're ready, unlike . . ." she blushed, "I guess you could say . . . some people I know."

"Well," I answered, "that would be true only if you aren't tripping over it in the middle of the night. That happens to me fairly often, and let me tell you, it hurts plenty."

Yvonne laughed. "Yes, that happens sometimes to me too. I remember you always liked to think things through,

Bob, didn't you? I'm glad you haven't lost that. This is really good cake, by the way. I know it's rude to ask, but do you suppose Dee Dee could have another piece? Look at the way she's inhaled this one. This is the first nice thing that's happened to her all day."

"Of course," I said. I went into the kitchen to cut Dee Dee another slice, as well as one for her mother.

When I returned I handed the cake to Yvonne. Dee Dee had picked up the pen again and was writing her name on the arm of the couch. "Don't worry," I told Yvonne. "If there's anybody who knows how to remove that kind of thing, it's me."

"Thanks," she said. "This cake is so light and fluffy, plus there's something I can't identify, earthy, but also full of perfume, not sweet, but with its own flavor. These little seeds, are they what I think they are?"

"They're fennel," I said, and I noticed that several small yellow cake crumbs had settled pleasantly on the tops of Yvonne's tanned breasts.

Dee Dee finished her second piece, wiped her mouth, and held out her plate for a third. The cake seemed to have settled her down. I brought her another piece even though her mom gave her a stern look.

Dee Dee finished her cake. "Well," Yvonne said, "I'm really sorry you don't know anyone who owns a fair-sized brown dog, but we certainly thank you for the cake. I'm sure the cake has helped Dee Dee feel much better, hasn't it, Dee Dee?"

Her daughter nodded again and, looking at her feet, suddenly turned shy. Yvonne rose to walk to the door and Dee Dee followed, reluctantly, I thought.

Before she reached the door, however, Yvonne paused. "You're sure you don't know anything about a dog?"

I shook my head.

"Well," she said, "you've been so kind. I only wish I had something to repay you with." Then she closed her eyes. "Wait," she said, "I just now thought of a poem for you, and if you have a piece of paper, maybe even a cocktail napkin, I could write it down. For some reason, napkins seem to help. It's not real haiku, strictly speaking, though I think it's in the spirit of haiku, brevity-wise."

I brought her a paper towel. She wrote something and then looked it over.

"OK," she said, "here goes":

Looking for a vicious dog
I find my past with—
A touch of fennel!

"No kidding," I said. "I'd say that over the past years your talent has developed considerably, even if it isn't a real haiku."

"I'm glad you like it," Yvonne said. "I'm fairly sure it still needs a little work. It's just a first draft, and if I've learned anything, it's that writing is really a hard business. Some of my customers at the casino have told me they find my poems just a bit too contemporary for their tastes, but I think this one makes a personal statement, don't you?"

"I certainly do," I told her. "I'm really glad to see you again. And speaking of seeing you again, let me give you my card." I handed her a card that read BOB'S UPHOLSTERING, and underneath it, *Re-cover the Past*, followed by my address and my phone number. "If you need anything re-covered, or just want to talk about the good times we had together, feel free to call."

"Thanks," she said. "So long. And good luck with your invention, even though you haven't invented anything yet."

And so I watched as the two of them strode together down the front walk to the busy street, reentering their world of uncertainty and hurt. Perhaps, I thought, in the very next block they'd find the true culprit who had nipped young Dee Dee, and it would turn out not to have been poor Bob at all, but some treacherous terrier or truculent chow. And then, when Yvonne confronted the biter's owner, that person, stung by guilt and shame, would settle on Dee Dee a generous annuity for the rest of her life, or at least through college. Or maybe Dee Dee would skip college, at least for a while, as so many young women do, in order to start a family of her own.

No doubt mother and child would continue their quest, I thought, if only for an hour or two, knocking on doors, including Farley's (who wasn't home), ringing doorbells in search of someone to blame. *Should* I run down the walk after them and say something like: "Oh, I just remembered. You said you were looking for a *live* dog, but if a dead one would help out I happen to have one buried in my backyard that you can take a look at"? It wasn't too late, but then, what kind of a person would she think I was?

Be strong, I told myself. *Resist. If you want even a prayer of a chance to resume a meaningful relationship with this lovely woman again, keep your mouth closed, at least until they are out of sight.*

I looked at the Communicator once again. The dog was right. I needed to get back to my real work one of these days, and soon.

7

I waited for Yvonne to call, but she never did. Days passed, and gradually I turned my thoughts back to the Communicator. Somehow, my practically back-to-back meetings with Bob and Yvonne had made its development that much more urgent. Every couple of hours, I would pick it up and shake it around, but I could hear nothing that sounded in the least like a dead person talking, only the usual static and clicks— no advice, no cries for help—nothing. Sometimes I took it to bed with me and lay next to it, as if it were a wife, until I fell asleep. I couldn't even say what I was expecting.

One night, I was watching a television special about polar bears being hunted from low-flying planes. As the bears walked around on their ice floes, suddenly—*bam!*—a hunter would shoot them, and his pilot would radio a boat to pick up the corpses or, more frequently, to remove only the skins for trophies and leave the bloody carcasses behind. Afterward, the floe would melt into nothing. In a couple more decades, nudged along by the itchy trigger-finger of global warming, every polar bear on earth would be dead, except for those in zoos. At the end of the program there was a telephone number people could call to pledge money to stop these terrible acts. I wrote the number down. Those bastards, I thought, they *have* to be halted before it's too late, and I was about to pick up the receiver and make a pledge when it occurred to me that even if I called immediately, these acts had already happened. It already *was* too late, not only for those dead bears on the show but probably also for all the bears left in the world, and the tigers, elephants, and giraffes as well. Would a person ever be able to undo all the damage mankind had done?

I made my way into the backyard. The rosebush looked healthier, even in the dark.

I stood there in front of the bush and spoke. "Bob," I said, "I'm feeling unbelievably bad right about now."

There was a rumble in the distance—maybe thunder, though it didn't feel like rain—and the rosebush seemed to answer in a voice that, because it was deep and a little throaty, I figured could be Bob's. It said, "Hey, lighten up, friend. Take a walk; I can't promise anything, but if there's one thing I know about, it's walks, and they sure used to help me whenever I was a little down."

"Bob," I said, "is that you?"

There was no answer.

Why not? I thought. At least taking a walk was a plan.

I went back inside the house and pulled on a light jacket, just in case the air grew colder, then stepped out the front door. The sound of the lock's click was louder than I expected, and I looked around to see if anyone else had heard it, but none of my neighbors, including the guy across the street, even had their lights on. As for Farley, he was either at home or at work; I couldn't tell for certain. I turned back to stare at my house for a minute. The asphalt shingles on the roof, even in the dark, looked patchy, and someday soon the whole outside was going to need a good paint job; there were blistered spots, and places where I could see bare wood. I wondered how my place of residence had appeared to Yvonne as she stood outside my door before I opened it, and I had an odd sensation. Standing there, outside my house, looking at it, I fancied for a moment that I had never left, that I was still inside, going about my business, maybe putting a strip of leather along the top of a chair's armrest, or possibly doing nothing but watching television, a nature show. So now there were two of me, and the me who was standing outside my house had become the stranger, someone I had yet to be introduced to, while the me inside, the one watching a program on squirrels, the familiar me, I couldn't get back to.

Around the outside me, slabs of sidewalk glowed dimly beneath the street lamps like squares on a game board that spread in all directions. There wasn't a moon, and the overhanging branches of trees alternately blocked or revealed the sky, itself faintly aglow with the lights of the city and stars stuck here and there. In which direction would the stranger who was me wander? There was nowhere in particular I needed to go, of course, so I turned left and headed down the street, unconsciously tracing in reverse what might have been Bob's last journey. As I walked, I could hear the shush of leaves and the occasional faint crunch of a snail beneath my feet. It seemed as if I were the only person awake, an arrow loosed by the hand of destiny from a gigantic bow and speeding toward a target too far away to see.

In any case, Bob had been right; the night air made me feel better, and I walked with a vigor I hadn't felt in years, as if the air I sucked into my lungs included some sort of chemical additive containing unimaginable amounts of energy—invisible, of course, and possibly dangerous. If there hadn't been the potential hazards of obstacles—broken slabs of sidewalk, monkey balls dropped from trees, discarded children's toys, and fallen branches—I might even have begun to trot.

I walked faster, oblivious to where the he who was I was headed. I passed a house I was sure I'd passed before, and a little while later I shook my head disapprovingly over the same abandoned Chevy Suburban I thought I had shaken my head disapprovingly over earlier that night. I turned a corner that it seemed I'd turned twice already, and then, as in the dream I'd had about the warehouse, I was completely lost.

I passed rows of houses, alley after alley (there are few cities with more alleys than St. Nils, but why, I have never been able to determine). Finally, after an uphill stretch that must have lasted three blocks, I found myself short of breath. I leaned against a sturdy trash can in an unfamiliar alley and waited to recover.

The trash can smelled strongly of fish and my right side ached. I tried to locate where I was. I thought I knew the neighborhood—it was impossible I could be *that* lost—but most of the houses that lined the alley had fences too high to allow the observation of anything besides an upper story, and, besides, their lights were off. Looking through a space between the boards of a high wooden fence straight into the building across from me, a duplex, I spotted a yellowy gleam from what must have been a first-floor kitchen, because in the background I could see a refrigerator, complete with a child's drawing (what looked to be a cat beneath dark clouds of rain, and possibly a waffle) and various scraps of paper stuck here and there. The ache in my side turned to curiosity. Somebody other than me was still awake, but who could that person be?

A stack of four square, plastic crates, the kind used to carry milk, was next to the trash can. I removed one of the crates, using it as a step to stand atop the trash can, and peered over the fence.

The warm, yellow light of the window created a sort of timeless feel, like the effect of an exhibit I once saw at the Museum of Natural History, one that included a family of Inuit squatting by a dead polar bear. This had been a rough night for polar bears, come to think of it, but in the frame before me were no Inuit and no bears; there was only a single woman wearing a worn, purple velour bathrobe. Her back was to me, and she was seated at her kitchen table, her right arm moving as if she were writing something on a piece of paper. Every so often, she would take a sip from a sturdy, steaming mug, scratch her head, then write some more.

She turned her face and I saw it was Yvonne. I realized the drawing taped messily to the refrigerator behind her must be Dee Dee's, just as those taped-up scraps of paper must be the phone numbers for babysitters and for parents of Dee Dee's classmates. Was my business card there, too? I couldn't tell. Dee Dee would be sleeping peacefully in her room by now, her arm healed, dreaming whatever dreams little girls had these days. Meanwhile, Yvonne had taken out her braids and tied her hair back into the ponytail I remembered from our time together at the institute, but obviously she was having a tough time sleeping. Every so often she would hold her head in her hands, then lift her head and shake it, as if she were preparing to face some enemy. Was she worried about money? Was Dee Dee's absent father pressing Yvonne in some way? Who was he anyway, and why *hadn't* Yvonne called me? Maybe I should have gotten her number—"In case I happen to run across that dog," I could have told her.

All around me the night was absolutely silent. Five, ten, fifteen minutes passed. My left leg was starting to grow numb. At last Yvonne rose, finished her beverage, rinsed the mug, and left it in the sink. She shut off the light.

A minute later an upstairs light came on, but now a half shade obscured the lower part of what looked to be a bathroom window. Luckily, I was able to swing a leg up from the trash can lid to balance for a moment on the top of the fence and, using an overhanging branch to climb into an adjacent tree, move to a better position for viewing. My leg, which had started to cramp, felt better, too, and once I got settled I could see that Yvonne certainly *was* in a bathroom, standing in front of the mirror, holding a toothbrush in her right hand, a barely squeezed tube of toothpaste in the other, her left.

Her toothpaste I recognized as the same one she had used back when I first knew her, a brand I still used myself, one advertised to have "improved whitening power." It was a fresh tube, so she must have gotten it recently, unless, of course, she was the sort of person who bought things on sale in quantity and stored them until she needed them. Had she always been like that or had the misfortunes of life forced her to be that way? There were so many questions I wanted to ask I didn't know where to start.

Her teeth brushed, Yvonne leaned closer to the mirror. Was she really seeing herself, I wondered, or her daughter's smaller, near-identical face? Whoever Dee Dee's father was, as nearly as I could see he hadn't made much of an impression on the features of his daughter's face. Where *was* the dad, anyway? Had he met an untimely end or only left for greener pastures, though what pasture could be greener than Yvonne's? I certainly had found none.

"Yvonne, it's me, Bob. If you need a hand, you know where I live," I wanted to call out, but then she turned toward me and I could see that her purple robe was fastened only loosely by a sash that was nearly coming undone. Her breasts were fuller than I recalled, and the branch I was sitting in gave an unsettling creak.

Yvonne paused. Had she heard it, too? She must have, because, pulling her robe closed, she walked to the window and stared out into the dark. What did she see? Surely not me, hidden as I was by leaves and branches, nor the alley hidden by the fence, nor her hidden future, as troubled as it seemed to be. But as much as I wanted to be there for her at that moment, I thought that this would not be the best way for us to reconnect.

The bathroom light went out. Not wanting to startle her, I waited a few minutes without moving, and only then did I drop down from the tree, pulling out my back in the process. It was torture to walk, but by moving in a sort of rigid, jerky motion, I actually made enough progress so that I managed to travel a whole three blocks by the time the patrol car glided up behind me, its lights turned off.

Then a policeman carrying a long metal flashlight stepped out to join me on the pavement. "We got a call about a prowler," he said. "You wouldn't happen to know anything about that, would you, pal?"

8

Still testing. One, two. What the heck . . . My name is Dee Dee, and I'm wondering if anybody out there is out there.

9

The police officer standing behind the flashlight was about my weight, though shorter, and probably about twenty years older than me. On a scale of physical fitness I would have to call him a six, while I was probably a four, ten being the highest. On his uniform shirt, above the silver name tag that read "Steadman," there looked to be a dried spot of taco sauce, though it was hard to identify it in the dark. The lettering on his tag was the same unimaginative black-on-silver-background that you always see on cops. Once, a few years ago, I tried to improve the quality of life in St. Nils by writing a letter to the police department proposing that hand-lettered name tags, individually selected by each officer and personalized with pictures of kittens, puppies, or even their kids, would go a long way toward humanizing members of the force in the eyes of a skeptical public. I never got an answer.

In response to the flashlight-holding lawman's question about whether I was in possession of any information concerning a prowler, I explained that I had been watching a special about polar bears being shot from small planes for no reason at all. I added that I had found it extremely upsetting, and so in order to settle down I had decided to take a walk around the neighborhood to see if I could find some inner peace. I left out the part about the talking rosebush.

"Inner peace?" he said. "Are you telling me you're walking around in the middle of the night to find inner peace?"

It appeared I wasn't getting through, so I went back to his playbook: "A prowler? No, officer. I haven't seen anyone. I was just heading home to go back to bed when you stopped me." I smiled. "I wish I could help find whomever it is you're looking for, but truthfully, it's been completely quiet out here. I haven't come across a single other person."

Steadman looked me up and down with something that may have been empathy, but which was probably closer to contempt. A lot closer. "Don't try to make a run for it," he said. Then he walked slowly back to the patrol car and entered the particulars of my identification, which I had handed to him, into his computer. While he waited for the computer to respond, I stretched my back as best I could and looked around to see if any of the neighbors' lights were on. They weren't. Either they were all sound sleepers or this sort of middle-of-the-night encounter was more common than I imagined. From far away I could hear the distant howl of a dog. After what seemed like a very long while, Steadman returned with my identification.

"The computer's down again so maybe we should just talk," he said. "Besides, I'm usually a pretty good judge of character in matters such as this. According to your address, you're not all that far away from your house. How long do you claim you've lived in this neighborhood?"

I told him. He looked me over once again and shrugged. "OK. Get in. We'll talk where it's more comfortable. Is your back sore or something? If not, how come you're walking as if it is?"

I explained that I had a back condition, and my doctor had ordered me to take moderate exercise, such as walking when the streets weren't too crowded. "He was afraid that someone might jostle me," I said.

Steadman nodded. "No telling about backs," he said. "Your doctor is right; you do have to be careful." Then he pointed to the waiting squad car, which in itself did not inspire confidence. There was tree sap covering its hood, roof, and trunk, and the front end was a mass of vicious-looking dents, large and small. On the fender of the passenger's side someone had scratched the word *PIG*.

Steadman opened the passenger door and moved aside a Styrofoam carton holding what was left of an order of sweet-and-sour ribs. "You sit in front. Watch your head getting in."

I sat next to him gingerly. Modern police cruisers are virtual cockpits of high-tech radio equipment, computers, and weaponry, but in that one, at the moment, an easy-listening station was playing an upbeat version of "Moon River." Steadman reached over and switched it off. "Sorry," he said. "Driving around like this late at night, I've gotten into the habit of listening to this stuff. I know not everybody likes it, but it's good for the long haul. I'd like to see the kids these days when they're sitting in their old folks' homes in their wheelchairs, trying to click their arthritic fingers, rapping about being a gangsta and yelling at their bitches, who'll be in pimped-out wheelchairs, I suppose. I tell you, it makes me smile. Sorry about those polar bears, by the way." Maybe it was being inside his car, but his whole demeanor had become a lot friendlier.

Steadman had smallish eyes, and a face that looked as if someone had grabbed him by his ears and pulled backward very, very hard; he resembled, now that I thought of it, a polar bear. It wasn't an unattractive look, just not one I was used to seeing every day. From where I sat I noticed a large mole, like an aerial photograph of an igloo, resting on the right side of his cheek. "Are you employed?" he asked me.

I handed him a business card.

"Married?"

"No."

"Family?"

"No."

"Me, either." Steadman paused and fixed his gaze through his windshield at a fresh spot of something on the hood of the squad car. In the dark it was hard to make out its exact composition. "Tell me, do you ever get lonely?"

I looked at him. He had a piece of green lint above his right ear, and I wondered if he was trying to trick me in some way. Did they teach this stuff at the police academy—something like "show vulnerability and gain the confidence of the perpetrator"?

"Well, sure," I answered. "But it's not like it's anyone's fault, officer . . ."

"You can call me Steadman," he said.

On the other hand, was he coming on to me? I looked at the man again. It didn't seem possible. I continued, "That's a tough one, Steadman. Sure, my customers sometimes invite me to parties—birthdays and the like—store grand openings, wedding anniversaries, you know, and sometimes they take me to meetings of their clubs or church groups, but I know what they're thinking. They're thinking, 'Bob's an all right guy. He doesn't look so bad—he looks, I don't know, come to think of it, like some kind of animal, but I don't know what kind. All he needs is a little nudge to meet nice people, and he'll be one of us. Then, if he does turn out to be my friend, maybe later on down the line in a couple of weeks or so I can ask him as a favor to redo, at no charge, that old Morris chair that's been stored in my attic forever.'"

"*Your* attic?"

"Well, their attics. So I go to their parties and their gatherings, and they *are* nice people. They talk about celebrities, or sports teams, or the stock market, but, frankly, it all seems kind of trivial when you put it against the really major questions of life and death and the relationship between these two states of being. I used to be a student at the Institute for Mind/Body Research, which didn't really have a sports team, or many business courses, for that matter, so I never really got all that much into sports and business."

Steadman stared at me with a peculiar expression.

"In other words," I continued, "I go to all these places, and I'll be talking with someone or another when I think, I've listened to them gas on about their favorite vacation, or their cat, or whatever, so now it's my turn. 'Hey,' I say to them, 'what are your feelings about the possibility that one day we may be able to communicate with the dead? Does that sort of thing interest you?'"

Steadman's expression shifted slightly, but I couldn't tell quite where it was headed.

"Or," I went on, "maybe I ask them what sort of messages they plan to send, once they are dead, to those who are left behind, and, if they're thinking they can give advice to their loved ones, why would they believe anyone would follow it any more than advice they might give right now?

"Then the person, whoever it is, will look at me. 'Say,' they'll tell me. 'Have you tried that dip over there? I just can't keep away from it, myself.' Then they're walking off. So I'll wait for a couple of minutes for them to come back and when they don't, I walk to the nearest corner, make my way along a wall toward an exit, and before I know it, I'm out the door. But don't feel sorry for me; that's just the way it is."

It occurred to me that Steadman had a rare ability to get people talking. I could see why he was a successful cop, if he was.

Steadman looked as if he were considering what I had just told him. "The Institute for Mind Body Research, huh? Do you really think it's as simple as that, by which I mean being stuck in that old dualistic world? Wouldn't you say instead that we have a body, and one of the attributes of that body just happens to be thought, along with eating, and belching, and screwing, and picking your nose? You don't see people starting Institutes of Mind slash Nose Picking, do you? Or Mind slash Blow Jobs?" He released the cruiser's parking brake. "You seem like a decent guy, though, so suppose I give you a ride home."

I thought for a moment about reminding him that while the mind is just a part of the body, it's also the only part of the body capable of naming itself and, as such, the only part that can reflect on its role vis-à-vis the body. In other words, isn't the mind the only entity in the entire world that can stand in active opposition to the body, much as it was the job of Satan to stand up against God? I said none of this, however, in part because I was happy to have the strain off my back, and in part because I didn't want to say anything that might encourage any of the man's authoritarian tendencies. Instead, I watched as the darkened houses moved by us as in a dream, though not a particularly restful one, because Steadman wasn't the best driver in the world.

Then the mole on Steadman's cheek throbbed for a minute and his voice dropped a note, surprising me. "The Institute for Mind Body Research . . . huh? I wish that when I was younger someone would have founded an institute that explored the interrelationship between crooks slash the law. I would have liked to attend a place like that once upon a time—who wouldn't? Let me tell you, Bob, this policeman's life is not as rewarding as you might have come to believe from watching television. It's not all gun battles and hostage dramas. Do you have any idea what it's like to have to drive around the city alone night after night, the only individual awake when practically everybody else is sleeping, including the real criminals, those very people who in general are at the heart of ninety-nine percent of your gun battles and hostage situations?

"So what do I get? I get the smash-and-grab geniuses at the local liquor store, the teenage hoodlums using their el-cheapo screwdrivers made in China to pry a stereo from a dashboard (though for some reason that particular crime seems to have diminished of late); I get the kids in parked cars making out, their windows steamed and their cars trembling with their passion; or, conversely, I wind up chasing after the Peeping Toms and stalkers—not even real criminals at all, just deviants or opportunists who, for one reason or another, can't manage to find a place for themselves in the world of white-collar crime, where ninety-nine percent of the perpetrators go unpunished. And don't get me started on stockbrokers. If you think you can have a meaningful conversation with scum like that, can settle down and have a pleasant chat with them such as you and I are having now about the finer things in life, you've got another thing coming. Mind slash body—sure."

The patrol car turned right and ran slightly up over a curb.

"Fucking curbs," said Steadman. He readjusted himself behind the wheel, as if that would fix it. "Do you have any idea at all how humiliating it is to have to pull into an empty convenience store parking lot just for a little late-night communication with a low-paid clerk who only wants you out of there so he can resume playing his Game Boy or return to reading his comic book—*graphic novel*, they like to call them these days—*novel*, my foot—don't get me started in that direction, either, or I won't shut up. Are you a reader, Bob? You look like one."

"I guess you could say I've read a few books," I told him. We made a quick left and drove down an unfamiliar alley.

"A shortcut," Steadman explained.

"In other words, can you even imagine how few people I meet in the course of an evening who are willing to discuss anything so complex as the concepts inherent in that question of which came first, the chicken or the egg? Talk about a tree falling in a forest! Let me tell you, Bob, serious discussion is the last thing a pervert wants to engage in, believe me, and while, sure, there are a few intellectually curious patrolmen at the station house these days—certainly more than there used to be in the past, a situation I attribute—don't laugh—to the proliferation of crime shows on television—a lot of good that is to those of us who have to drive the streets to make a living."

We arrived at my house.

"Well, here we are," Steadman said. "I must say I've enjoyed talking with you. Maybe we'll have a chance to do it again some night in the future."

"Yes," I said, with my hand on the handle of the car door, "that would certainly be great."

I spent the rest of the night, all the way into the morning, working feverishly on the Communicator and getting nowhere fast.

10

Finally, when it was nearly dawn, I rubbed some analgesic balm on what I could reach of my back and got ready for bed. Around me was the usual smell of leather, a hill of dirty dishes in the kitchen and, in my bedroom, on the wall, the poster that Yvonne had given me of the roads built by those Roman bullies of long ago, roads shoveled over by the peace and quiet of the Dark and Middle Ages and then excavated by the busybodies of the last two centuries. One day Yvonne would be surprised to know that I had kept the poster after all these years, but I didn't want to scare her off by telling her the news too soon.

I crawled into bed and thought about Yvonne while I waited for the balm's heat to diminish. I wouldn't be re-covering any furniture for at least a day, maybe two. Mean-while, visions of Yvonne at her kitchen table, of her standing before the bathroom mirror, of her turning to look out her window into the night replayed in my mind. I remembered how Yvonne herself—her back so straight it pushed her chest invitingly forward—had sat in this very house next to Dee Dee as the two of them rested on my couch, eating their pieces of cake, only a room away from the bedroom I cur-rently occupied. I lay in bed and imagined how the two of them must have returned to their duplex afterward, a little tired and probably grumpy, Yvonne bending over, tucking Dee Dee into bed so her daughter could sleep through her mom's next shift waitressing at the casino.

"But it's still light out, Mommy," Dee Dee would have said.

"Yes, but wasn't it nice of that man to give us all that delicious cake. His name is Bob. Mommy knew him a long while ago, before you were born, and come to think of it, Dee Dee, Mommy may well have misjudged him." Then Yvonne would have added, "Fennel—that Bob is certainly full of surprises. And doesn't thinking about that cake make you feel better?"

So Dee Dee would have nodded, a little uncertain, admitting to herself what a nice man that Bob had been, promising herself that the next time she saw him—which she hoped would be soon—she would try to act nicer.

Finally Yvonne would kiss her daughter's forehead. "Now go to sleep. Your birthday's coming soon." (*Was* it her birthday? I didn't know, but it sounded good.) "What would you like for a present? Nothing too expensive, mind you! And would you like to invite Bob to your party?"

"Yes, that would be fun, and maybe he can bring us more of that good cake, Mommy. Oh, and can I invite my father, too? I'd like to meet him one day soon."

"Your father," Yvonne possibly would have answered, "I'm afraid he's long gone, honey. But that's a very good idea of yours to invite Bob. Now, where did I put that card he gave me? I know it's around somewhere . . ."

What would it be like to have a stepdaughter? It might not be bad at all, I thought. Furthermore, I was running out of hope with women. The truth was, Yvonne had been my longest relationship ever, and in all the years since I had last seen her there had been only three others. The first, Marlene, was an Animal Technician One at the local shelter, and we lasted exactly four dates. "Sit and stay," she told me after I finished paying for our last meal of chicken-fried steak and French fries, and had gotten up to follow her out the door. "I won't be hearing from you again, you understand?" I supposed by now she might be an Animal Technician Two, or even Three.

The second, Jody, told me to stop calling her right after I had re-covered a complete living room set and the seats of two mission armchairs for her. The last, Tina, never told me anything at all, but the day I walked into a coffee shop and saw her in a corner snuggling with a one-armed man, I realized our relationship had no future.

The pain in my back was starting to ease a bit; I got out of bed and turned on the television to relax. The me who had stayed at home and the one who had left were finally joined together again.

It was very close to dawn, though dawn hadn't arrived just yet. Instead of the prime-time nature programs that showcased poisonous reptiles or large, dangerous animals, all I could find was a special on the noises made by various living things, and it was a program I'd seen before, but had shut off after the first few minutes. This time I left it on and tried to doze. It almost worked, too, but then, just as I was falling asleep, something caught my half-closed eyes. The program turned to the surprising sounds made by plants and animals that we don't ordinarily hear, but which are all around us. In order to listen to these barely audible sonic emissions, the scientists created what they described as "a nearly perfect soundproof environment" by covering the walls of a room with egg cartons. Then they stuck whatever fish, or bug, or mammal they wanted to listen to inside the room along with a highly sensitive microphone, and stood outside getting the sounds down on tape. The results were amazing: fish crashed around in their fishbowls, plants moaned, and a particular strain of acidophilus gave off a chord in G minor.

I thought about it. Suppose, I asked myself, the dead *were* trying to communicate with us all the time but, just as over the last hundred years or so, light pollution has pretty much blocked our view of the stars, so noise pollution is blocking out the Terminal Waves? In other words, all our prized automobiles, airplanes, and lawn mowers, our iPods and televisions playing at the same time, not to mention everyone on earth yelling into cell phones and expressing their half-baked opinions on radio call-in shows, have, over the last couple of hundred years, but especially of late, created a practically impenetrable layer of sonic interference that blocks our ability to receive anything other than our own pathetic daily emanations, estranging us from all who went before.

What had been missing from my earlier experiments with the Communicator was a soundproof room. But I didn't have an extra room in my house that I could turn into a sound lab, and even if I covered the bathroom, the smallest room in my house, coating the walls completely in cartons, the number of eggs I'd have to eat would be staggering. And then I had another thought: I didn't need to cover an entire room in cartons; I only needed to build a space large enough to enclose my own head. All that was necessary was to create a soundproof bubble I could slip on and off over headphones. I considered the concept: It seemed a relatively simple task to construct a sort of outer layer, in the form of a helmet, roughly in the shape of a diving bell, but made entirely out of egg cartons with some glue and duct tape to hold the cartons together. It would block from my immediate hearing all the random noises that are a part of living every day, leaving behind only those picked up by the directional microphone, then—voila!—once I got it pointing in the right place, there I'd be, hearing the voices of the dead with everything else more or less stuck inside a parenthesis. Watching that television show had made me feel foolish for having relied all those years on the so-called high technology of noise-blocking headphones, but such, I knew, was the way of scientific progress. Given all the centuries of sonic interference that I was dealing with here, I considered myself a lucky guy to have gotten any solution at all so quickly.

But first, I had to reason things through. As far as the physical factors went, the number of egg cartons a person could carry wrapped around his head was limited, not only by the weight of the cartons but also by the fact that a person would have to be careful not to bump into doorways and the like.

In the second place, this same person would have to pay close attention where he or she aimed the sensitive microphone. To inadvertently train it on a jackhammer could easily destroy a person's eardrums in a moment. Certainly, before any mass production of the helmet actually began, I would have to consult a personal-injury lawyer to design a waiver for ear damage that would stand up in court. I also understood I would still have to discover the correct balance between letting the Terminal Waves in and protecting myself from the non-Terminal Waves that filled up the world—not as easy, I knew, as it sounded.

The next step was to buy some eggs.

When I returned from the market, I took the eggs (there were a lot of them) out of their cartons, put them into three large bowls, and placed them in the refrigerator. Then I spread out some pages—the front page and the society section—of the *St. Nils Eagle*, sat down on the floor, and got to work gluing the cartons together, using a small ottoman as an armature. It didn't take long, partly because my profession had already given me a fair amount of practice gluing things.

When the helmet was finished, I studied it for a while. The effect was similar to an advertisement featuring the head of a spokesman for a large chain of fast-food restaurants whose smooth and macrocephalic noggin is five or six times normal size. Mine, however, given the varied textures of the coarse egg cartons as they contrasted with the glossy silver of the duct tape, created a far more complex visual message, rugged and expressive, technologically sophisticated and yet homespun, masculine and yet feminine as well, in that it had been fabricated solely from containers for . . . well . . . *eggs*.

While I waited for the glue to dry (I knew from experience you can't rush these things), I plugged in the audio monitor I'd bought at Ed's Discount Electronics and spent several minutes making various unusual noises and striking parts of various household objects—tables, lamps, and so on—to compare how each one affected the swing of the needle. Then I hooked up the oscilloscope I'd also bought from Ed's and spent rather more time than I'd intended just watching the waves on its round screen. Each wave was a different size and shape, yet similar, in a way, to members of the same family—a mother and a daughter, for example—splashing in a wading pool. The waves were peaceful for now, and why not? Little did they suspect my goal was to eliminate them altogether with the flat line of brain death, of heart failure, of lung collapse, of silence, to push these inoffensive and yet bothersome waves out of the pool entirely in order make room for all the Terminal Waves that were, I hoped, struggling to break through to the surface.

At last I judged that the glue had completely dried and it was time to try out the helmet. I picked it up and carefully slid it over my head, noticing immediately that I had forgotten to make a space to look out of. I removed it, went to the kitchen, found a knife, and made a slit. Then I cut up a plastic bottle of diet cola to put over the slit to make a window so I could see where I was going. I glued the piece in place and covered the edges where it was stuck to the cartons with duct tape. The helmet *was* larger than I had wanted it to be, but not so large as to make walking around with it completely impossible. To help the matter, I found a handle from a broken end table drawer and glued it onto the outside to make it easier for me to carry.

When this second round of gluing was completed, I put the headphones on, and then lowered the helmet onto my head once again. It was hot and dark inside the helmet, and not very comfortable, though the good news was that even with the slit, things were pretty quiet, sound-wise. The bad news was that, for whatever reason, instead of tuning in to the helpful or sad monologue of a dead person (Could they hear me? I would have to wait to find out.), all I could hear—and faintly at that—was a distant howl. Or maybe it wasn't a howl at all, but I'd started to develop the first stages of tinnitus.

I removed the helmet and stared at it. I felt like stout Cortez silent on a peak in Darien, like Michelangelo and Jackson Pollack rolled into one as they stood before the blank canvases of what they surely knew were going to wind up as masterpieces worth millions. Was it possible, unbeknownst to me after all these years, that my mind, having been impregnated so long ago by Howard Bonano, had been busily gestating behind my back and now was about to give birth?

It occurred to me that it wouldn't hurt to give the whole thing a couple of coats of shellac—just in case I was outside with it and a sudden storm came up—not that the cartons couldn't be replaced fairly easily. I brushed on the shellac and looked at the helmet as it rested, glistening on the pages of the *Eagle*. I went to the kitchen and made myself a Spanish omelet, adding a few capers for extra flavor. I ate, washed the dishes, and then settled down to watch a show about starfish—typical midmorning fare.

Most of a starfish's life seems to be spent without such concerns as I had, and yet, what was death like for a starfish, I wondered? When one of its limbs starts a new body, does the new self have any memories of good times, or, for that matter, bad ones that the old self had already experienced? To a starfish, what is gain and what is loss? Are we like starfish—each of us a limb that once upon a time was connected to some large, invisible body, but is now severed from that body by years and accident and mere noise?

11

Testing. Nothing. Testing. Nothing.

Testing.

Still nothing.

Well, here goes anyway, my thoughts, straight out into the whatever.

The color here: white white white with just a little bit of yellow-gray. The sound: a really high-pitched whine that only bothers me when I listen hard for it. The sense of touch: forget it. The taste: salty, I think, and a little on the sweet side. The smell: a big surprise—the slight odor of gasoline, mixed with Lysol Spring Garden Scent room freshener, the kind my mother used to buy, with just a touch of burnt toast, and—given the general boringness of this place—I have to say the smell is one of the real highlights of my day, though, sadly, only through the lack of practically anything else.

Did I say "day"?

It's just a habit and I didn't mean it.

The same goes for thinking of me as *me*, when, as far as I can tell, there is not actually a *me* here exactly, at least not one that I would recognize having a head and hands and feet.

So how am I able to smell if I don't have a nose?

A good question, and, honestly, I have no idea, unless I'm not actually smelling anything—if you can follow me here—and somehow the smells I mentioned (burnt toast, gas, air freshener) aren't actual smells, but instead smells that were already in my head back when I was still a baby inside my mother: the smell of no smell.

Is there anything at all that's all right here?

Not really. Unless it's that I won't have to get braces. I told my mom about a thousand times I didn't want to have somebody open my mouth and put metal inside, but she said it wasn't up to me and I'd be getting them for sure when I was older and she saved up the money. Which would take a while.

Dr. Martin said it was my *overbite*.

Is anybody listening to me?

I have no idea.

12

I lifted the helmet of the Communicator onto my work-bench, where it sat powerful and serene. "Through me," it seemed to radiate, "thou shalt receive the wisdom of the ages. Through me, what was lost shall be found; through me, thou shalt go from life to death and then return again. Nice work, Bob, though it certainly took you long enough, I'd say."

I covered it with the blue tarp again so it wouldn't attract undue attention and began to pick up the shellac-spattered newspaper from the floor. The Hornets, I saw, were in the playoffs again, and I noted that the World of Pets was having something it called "Parakeetmania." Then I came upon an article that stopped me cold. ST. NILS

HAS FIRST RABIES FATALITY was the headline, and the article went on to tell how an eight-year-old girl had been bitten by an unknown canine outside her mother's duplex and, because the treatment that might have saved her was begun too late, the girl had died of the disease. Her mother was described as "grief-stricken," and the article added that the daughter had enjoyed a promising career at St. Nils Elementary School, where she had been in the gifted program. The girl, of course, was Dee Dee, and though the article reported that Yvonne was considering legal action against the hospital, it added that apparently she had signed a paper releasing it from any liability.

Poor Dee Dee! And poor Yvonne! No wonder she hadn't contacted me! Her hands must have been full with the details of her daughter's illness and then, after that, her daughter's death. I tried to picture Yvonne wearing black and walking everywhere with dark circles under her eyes.

If only I could have been around to help her, I thought, but then I said to myself, "No, Bob, let her deal with her grief in her own way. You never really knew Dee Dee, even though you took the time to give her all that cake, so you can empower Yvonne by giving her the time she needs. No doubt she has enough on her mind at this moment." (I checked the date—the article was a week old.) "Listen, Bob, the best you can do is to be there for her when she emerges from the darkness back into the light. Don't hurry the process; wait until she reaches out to you, and, after she does, then you can give her the good news that thanks to the Communicator, she'll be speaking with Dee Dee again any day now."

I fell asleep.

Around midnight I was awakened by a knock at the door. I opened it to find myself staring once again into the extra-long, heavy-duty flashlight of Officer Steadman.

He said, "Good evening. The Park Ranger, I presume?"

"The what?"

"Oh," he answered. Clearly Steadman was disappointed. "I was kind of hoping you might react to that name. It just so happens that someone has been going around committing potentially serious crimes in St. Nils and leaving behind a series of long and threatening notes. He signs them 'The Park Ranger' and I was thinking there was an off chance you might just be that individual. If there's one thing I've learned in my years as a cop, it's that the human mind is strange. How's your back, by the way?"

"Much better, thanks. Crimes like what?"

"So far they're mostly fire-oriented," Steadman answered. "Trash cans, a vacant lot, somebody's storage shed, but these situations can be tricky. The actual psychological profile of a pyromaniac is known to students of criminal behavior as one of the least stable and most potentially dangerous of any lawbreaker. Such an individual can remain lucid, even witty, for long periods of time, fooling members of his own family and community, often occupying respectable positions and receiving the accolades of friends and colleagues—civic awards, too—then, all at once, he will erupt into a solid wall of flames. I say *he*, by the way, because it is a known fact that ninety-nine out of a hundred pyromaniacs are male."

"Well, I'm sorry. I'm not the Park Ranger," I said. "I never heard of him. I'm Bob, remember?"

"Of course you're Bob, Bob, and given that you claim not to

be the Park Ranger, in that case, you are lucky, because from the few clues we have, the Park Ranger isn't the sort of person you should open your door to, particularly late at night."

But if I *were* the Park Ranger, then how could I open the door to myself? I thought. Before I could pose this one to Steadman, he continued, "And speaking of walking around in the middle of the night, Bob, I hate to do this, but I'm going to have to ask you to accompany me on a short trip to the police station. Don't worry; I'll give you a ride back home when we're finished. It won't take long."

He paused to stick his head inside my front door and looked around. "What's all that stuff under that blue tarp on the table? You're not building a bomb or anything like that, are you? Just joking," he winked.

"Oh that," I said. "It's just a bunch of electronic equipment that I'm using to make a kind of stereo . . . you know . . . for listening."

Steadman pointed toward his squad car a half a block away to suggest we go there. He must have parked there in order to sneak up on my house; I had to commend his policing technique.

"Why?" I said.

"Don't worry," Steadman replied. "This is entirely a matter of routine police business. Just get inside the car and I'll take you downtown with me."

"Now?"

"Do you want me to take out a warrant?"

I told him I did not.

"Bob, you are a wise man," Steadman said. "Did you tell me how your back is these days? I forget."

The police station at night turned out to be an entirely different universe from the cigarette-butt-strewn, sweat-filled, tension-laden workplace of the day, crammed to the brim with the drama and tears of human experience that I and millions of other television viewers had come to expect and love from all those seasons of long-running cop shows whose characters, week after week, could be counted on to balance their personal problems with the needs of their communities and the petty whims of their superiors and liberal judges. Steadman held open the heavy front door of the station for me to enter, saying, as if to prepare me for a shock, "You'll have to excuse us. We're not exactly used to visitors at this hour."

"Yo, Marty," the desk officer said to Steadman as he approached. Then the man noticed me and appeared embarrassed to be caught carefully filling out a large cross-word puzzle while dressed in blue pajamas and a green plaid flannel bathrobe. He put down his mug of hot chocolate, a single half-melted marshmallow still floating on its surface. In a manner that bespoke authority, he inquired, "What seems to be the difficulty here?" He raised an arm, using his sleeve to wipe the ring of chocolate from around his mouth, and pushed the crossword out of the way. "Do either of you know a nine-letter word for *criminal*?"

"Doesn't *criminal* have nine letters?" I said.

"It has eight."

"*Malefactor*," said Steadman. "Don't worry, George," he continued. "This will only take a minute. I don't think what we have here is a hardened perp, exactly. He's more in the area of helping me out on a case." He playfully punched the desk officer in the shoulder and led me to the public reception area, a large room with high ceilings. Across the top had been strung a banner that read WELCOME HOME, BRAD, but whether it was meant for a returning officer or some likable recidivist, I couldn't tell. It could have been either, judging from the walls filled with signed wanted posters and the wooden benches covered with colorful throw pillows.

"It's a pity we can't leave those pillows out all the time," Steadman said. "They make the place look so much brighter, but the truth is that if we didn't pack them up before the start of the day shift, they'd be stolen. We don't always get the best class of customer around here, if you get my drift, but it's hard to blame them; they can't always help themselves."

We crossed the room, and Steadman nodded to various policemen using this quiet time to catch up on filling out their reports, to study for what appeared to be promotional exams, and even, judging by two cheerful-looking patrolmen who were carrying heaping baskets of clothes, to do their laundry. There was the smell of butterscotch cookies in the air. Here and there, policemen walked about carrying glasses of milk and plates of brownies. Off to one side, a guy with a few days' growth of beard and wearing a leather jacket—I guessed he was an undercover cop—worked, his brows furrowed, on a purple and brown macramé.

Leaving the common room, we walked down a corridor lined with cells. I listened to the pleasant snores of some of the prisoners sleeping in their cots, their blankets pulled up to their chins, while others, eyes shut, were being read to by officers sitting next to them atop naturally finished wooden stools. Steadman explained, "Contrary to much of what you might have heard, we policemen understand more than anyone the benefits to be gained by offering a stable and homelike atmosphere that most of these hardened criminals never had in their youth. Not only do they give us less trouble while they're here with us, but if for some reason they beat the rap and are set loose again by a permissive judiciary onto the streets, a high proportion of them go into jobs in the public-service sector, including nonprofits. In any case, it makes the whole business of picking them up again—if we have to—a lot easier. They tend not to put up much of a fight the second, or third, or fourth time around."

I slowed before a cell in which an officer was reading from a recent bestseller to a hairy-armed brute with what looked to be several fresh stitches in his skull. It so happened that I had recently finished the same book myself. It was the story of a man about to be executed for a crime he didn't commit despite the fact that he had committed several other equally reprehensible acts. Among the many questions the novel raised was, "Who among us is truly innocent?" The book's cover showed a man standing next to a gallows. The man was just a silhouette, but the gallows had a weird glow around it as if it were on fire. I recognized the selection he was reading as from the part where the main character, knowing his elderly next-door neighbor is allergic to peanuts, forces him to eat plate after plate of Pad Thai, pushing the old gentleman into anaphylactic shock and allowing the criminal to search the man's apartment from top to bottom for a stack of hidden Krugerrands.

Although the character had originally enjoyed watching the old man's subsequent wheezing, coughing, swelling of lips, paleness, bluish skin color, rapid pulse, sweating, fainting, and, finally, his complete unconsciousness, later, I knew from having finished the book, he would become tormented by repeated visions of his neighbor's death. For some reason an image of Farley refusing to hand over my overdue notice flashed before my eyes.

"I just finished that book myself, and you'll really like the ending," I said in answer to their questioning stares. I turned to Steadman. "This reading thing seems to have caught on."

"Yes," Steadman replied. "And the interesting thing is that most felons actually prefer novels to short stories or even poems, which was where we began this project. But the prisoners themselves tell us that the novels' longer narrative arcs give them a sense of continuity, as well as a chance, in a way, for them to escape their present unhappy circumstances, if only temporarily. As for their own writing, which we encourage through weekly workshops, they much prefer poetry. I don't know if it's a certain criminal lack of attention span—somebody ought to do a study one day—or just poetry's innate potential for violence and its implied permission to use inflammatory language, but they certainly do churn it out for whatever reason.

"And speaking of writing," Steadman continued, leading me to a door far in the back of the station that had the word INTERROGATIONS painted in gold letters on it, "this leads to the rooms where we question our suspects. There are several rooms inside and when one is vacant, it's not uncommon for an officer to come here during his break and make use of it either to get his thoughts in order by drafting a brief essay about whatever subject might be disturbing him, or to work on his memoir. In that regard, several of our rank have had considerable success in the field of the police procedural novel. I don't know if you've ever read *Down a Dangerous Street* by Ronald Willoughby, but that was written by one of the very officers you passed reading a bedtime book to a prisoner, and just last week he told me that a lucrative option has been taken out on it for a screenplay." Steadman opened another door. "I'm actually surprised to find this room free now, because his success has spawned a whole wave of imitators."

We passed into an interrogation room, more of a cubicle, in fact, than an actual room. It was well lit though sparsely furnished, with only two straight-backed chairs and an antique oak writing desk. I told Steadman I hadn't had an opportunity to read his colleague's novel, but I would certainly check it out from the library the first chance I got.

"Ah, the library. A lot of good that will do Willoughby. Royalties these days, as you well know, are small enough, but you can imagine what they shrink to if one book is read by a dozen cheapskates too tight to plunk down ten or twenty bucks for their own copy. Do you know how much a writer gets for a book? I myself was surprised to learn it's only ten or twenty percent, depending on the contract, so if a book sells, say, ten thousand copies—a really respectable number, by the way—how much does that come to? Practically nothing for a paperback, and maybe double that for a hardback, that's what. Do the math, Bob: there's computer paper, toner, countless cups of coffee, and also visits to the chiropractor because all that sitting at the keyboard isn't exactly a walk in the park for your spine. Then, out of that pitiful amount of royalty, ten or fifteen percent goes to the agent. I tell you, it breaks my heart. I hear these figures and I think these guys—even somebody as successful as Willoughby—must be crazy even to try. But you don't want to get me started on that, believe me. I have a little writing I'd like you to attempt yourself in a minute or so, but first I need to take your picture." Steadman reached over and took a grimy Polaroid camera from a low end table where it was resting by a vase of fresh-cut flowers.

I smiled and Steadman snapped the shutter. It was no better and no worse than other pictures taken of me over the years: brown eyes, a little wary; brown, thinning hair; an unshaved face with an unmistakable whiff of capybara about it; but still, a friendly face, and one wanting to help, to be of service. The face of a man who could be trusted to keep his word—even to a dog, if need be.

Then Steadman took out two sheets of ordinary white paper. The first had a set of phrases typed on it, and the other one was blank. "I'd like you to write the words on this first piece of paper I am giving you onto this blank sheet," he said, and he handed me a ballpoint pen. He clicked it so it would be ready to go. "Take your time," he said.

I looked at the list before me and copied:

>   Fruit jars
>   Jorney through life
>   Gouge

It may interest you to know
Burn
Make of what is left a sculpture from Hell
Weather permiting
Set fire to
Nor will those dolts in law enforcement
Greatful
Flammable
Quid pro quo
Respectfully yours

I didn't rush. I wanted it to be legible, but I didn't want it to appear that I was writing in any way that was different than usual. The last thing I needed was more late-night visits from Steadman. I handed both sheets back to him. "How's that?"

Steadman held the list up to the light and opened an envelope. Inside it was a handwritten copy of the same words and phrases he had just given me. He put the two sheets of paper together, one next to the other. "Well, I'm no expert, but offhand I'd say you are in the clear. We'll just keep what you wrote down in this file, together with this photo of you, and then if there's any trouble in the future we'll have everything set to go."

"Set to go?" I said.

He opened a drawer and put the file away. "Hang on," he said, closing the drawer. "I'll take you home in a minute. Just let me cancel my appointment with Carla, our massage therapist. Don't feel bad, though; she won't have any trouble filling it. After a few stress-related shootings a while back, the police commission wanted us to have a resident shrink. We tried it, but frankly a lot of us resented his prying into our pasts and the endless questioning about our feelings. Carla works out better for a lot of reasons. Plus, she says she's going back to college one of these days to be a psychologist, so basically we're getting the same thing, without the hassle and for much less money." We walked down another corridor. Steadman stuck his head into a room filled with soft light and scented oils; he said something over the sound of a pan flute.

We left the station, and on the ride home began a spirited discussion of whether criminals are born or made. Before we could come to any conclusion, however, I found the cruiser had stopped in front of my home.

"Another time, my friend," said Steadman.

13

OK, so I will just pretend somebody's listening. Here I am, Dee Dee, your reporter in the hereafter, which seems about the dumbest name I've ever heard for something that's already gone—I mean, shouldn't it be the *thereafter*? Or maybe the *aftermath*? And, yes, it *is* strange that an eight-year-old should use such fancy language, but, as near as I can tell, upon arriving, the first thing that happened was that I got a language upgrade—like a universal computer code, is how I think of it—and for a kid, at least, that means a free power-up in the vocab department. *Vocab* is what Miss Zachman calls it.

The trouble being if nobody else is here, why did I need an upgrade?

And if there *are* people around, why can't I see them?

I don't know.

Or maybe they're all talking to each other, but not to me.

And how many others are there?

That's another thing I don't know.

And I don't know who is responsible for the rules here, either.

Although I *can* tell you one thing, and that is I *do* feel pain, and a lot of it. I don't mean physical pain, naturally, but here the pain seems to be mostly about missing things. For example, I really, really miss (and once again I'm speaking here only for myself) all the things I left behind, like Lucky Charms, and those tennis shoes that light up when you walk, and my collection of glass cats in different colors. I have seven of them, and they all have jewels for eyes except one, which fell out. I also miss the corn dogs my mother used to make for me with the special corn dog machine she bought at a yard sale. It looks like a rocket ship.

And I miss my mom.

And PS: I know this is dumb, and even though I'm way too grown up for it now and I know it's only a baby show, I also miss *Tiny Alley* with Auntie June and Reckless Rabbit.

And PPS: I know I just said this, but I really, really, *really*, miss my mom.

Her name is Yvonne.

If you see her, tell her Dee Dee says hello.

Tell her Dee Dee loves her.

I have a dad, too, but I don't know who he is.

If anybody's listening.

14

What was going on? I'd lived in St. Nils all my life without any serious citizen-to-police interaction, and now, in the last couple of weeks, Steadman had shown up twice out of the blue. Was he in possession of some information I didn't have, or was it just plain dumb luck? "Routine police business," he'd said. I bet. I guessed Steadman must have been talking to that idiot, my neighbor Farley, and wondered if these visits had something to do with him.

That very next morning I took the tarp off the helmet. It was basically acorn-shaped, and roughly the size of a small ottoman (not a surprise, seeing as that's what I'd built it around). I'd had to leave the base of the neck large enough to fit over my head, so I hunted through the garage and found a ring of foam from an old seat cushion, inserting it along the opening to prevent chafing.

I put the tarp back over it and, while I thought about what to do next, I turned the television to *Zoo Brothers*, the story of twin brothers who work at the same zoo. One is really good and one is hopelessly evil. One of them is a keeper in the primate house and the other (the bad one) is the reptile keeper. The show was a favorite of mine, and a running theme was the argument between the two brothers over whose species—or whatever it was called—was superior. Also, the bad one played tricks on the good one. That morning, however, for some reason, the show couldn't hold my interest, though I left it on as I walked out to get the newspaper from the front porch. Next to the paper, beneath my welcome mat, I saw the corner of a medium-sized manila envelope sticking out.

I brought the envelope, along with the newspaper, back indoors, where the bad twin was stuffing a glob of lizard crap into one of his brother's rubber boots. He reminded me of Farley, but compared to the task I had ahead of me, I had to say that the concerns of the two brothers, as amusing as they'd been in the past, now seemed mostly trivial.

I shut the television off and went into the kitchen, where I made myself a pot of coffee and opened the paper: there was no more news of rabies, but a ferryboat had sunk, claiming over a thousand lives; the temperature of the earth was rising at an alarming rate, and members of the Republican Party were fighting to allow it to keep happening; human idiocy had finally got reason on the run, for sure. I finished the coffee and glanced over at the envelope. I'd assumed it held one of those flyers that advertise roof repair, handyman services, copper piping, and the like—all such offers, as far as I was concerned, being just another name for litter. I'd even tried it once myself: RECOVER YOUR FURNITURE, followed by my phone number. Two thousand flyers, and only three calls, all of them by addicts too stressed out to have gotten past the first word. This particular envelope, however, had my name written on it. I opened it.

Dear Bob,

Maybe you wonder how I know your name, or maybe, on the other hand, it might just be the most natural thing in the world that a person who was/is bent on avenging the death of his beloved pet would take the time, through a little elementary sleuthing, to discover that the name of his dog's killer happens (happened?—grammar's not my strong point) to be the same name as the dog I/he loved so much—possibly even too much, some say/said, including my/his court-appointed psychologist, Mandy.

But enough about me.

What about you, Bob?

What do you have to say for yourself?

Anything?

For you should know that Bob, as I had named my dog, was far more than just an animal to me, but instead nearly an extension of myself, the very embodiment—as Mandy says—of my subconscious desires and undefined personality. In other words, Bob, Bob was my inner child.

"And, surely, for a person to be in touch with his inner child is commendable," you might say.

Well, if you think I'm going to fall for that one, forget it. All you need to know is that though Bob was/is the embodiment of what I said before, he was also a real canine individual, one with a vibrant personality of his own. Bob was a dog, yes—but one with his own hopes and dreams, which I would watch him act out as he slept, running and getting nowhere because Bob liked to sleep on his left side, all the time letting out these little yips, or yelps, I guess you'd call them if you'd heard them.

But you didn't. I did.

Thus many were the hours I would sit on a chair in my kitchen and watch Bob as he lay there on the floor in front of the refrigerator, dreaming, and I would think: Is Bob yelping out of pain or pleasure? And now I'll never know simply because, Bob, through a selfish act of your own, you have managed to take the very name of Bob, and by virtue of the fact that it happens to be the same as your own, Bob, have turned bitter every pleasant association that repeating his name beneath my breath used to bring me, and might have continued to bring me in the future, had you not mixed into the mortar of his death your own, formerly sweet to me, now odious name, Bob.

I hope you are following this, Jerk Off.

So now, whenever I try to assuage my grief by remembering, for example, how much Bob liked to come along on my walks to the liquor store, the pharmacy, and the Medical Marijuana Express where I was working off a gift certificate from my mom, or how Bob would chase cats, stopping to lift his leg at practically every tree, all I can see is you, Bob's murderer, peeking out from behind one of those same trees, smirking at the awful deed you are/were about to perform. Forgive me, for what may be a confusing time element here. As a matter of fact, Mandy says that this continuing confusion between the past and present tense is at the root of all my problems. I'm trying to work it out, believe me.

Now back to the subject.

Likewise, Bob, when I think of how that other Bob would lift a paw, or sit, or stay (obedience school isn't cheap, Bob), and I would tell him, "Good Bob," now that very memory has been altered, so that instead of praising my dog I am forced to praise his murderer, you, and just how do you think that makes me feel, Bob?

I'm thinking you are getting the picture.

Mandy tells me it would be good if I abandoned this line of thinking, but obviously I disagree.

Because for me, Bob (you, not him), Bob (him, not you) was/is a part of me, though whether the good part or the bad part, I don't know—however, needless to say, Mandy has her own opinion about this matter, which she's only too happy to share, though, as far as I'm concerned, Bob, it's not all that important. What *is* important is that at the same time you murdered Bob, Bob, you therefore also killed a part of me, and, conversely, because a part of Bob is still in me, Bob, the fact that I am alive means that a part of Bob's alive as well also, to exact revenge for his untimely death. That is—if Bob wishes it so.

Dig it, as they say.

And therefore let me close, Bob, with a final question,

which is this: I assume that you (yes, you, Bob) are familiar with the great Russian novelist Fyodor Dostoyevsky, the author of *Crime and Punishment*, although I admit I have not actually gotten around to reading it myself at this juncture. In any case, it's my point here that those two words of his arguably most famous work go together like a horse and carriage, Bob, crime being the horse, and punishment the carriage that follows, the implication being that any individual, no matter how highborn or lowly, who has/had committed a dastardly crime cannot go unpunished. Also, that's what *Macbeth* was about, if I remember correctly from high school, or at least from those few days I actually went to English class, though since then I have come to be a great admirer of the literary arts. And speaking of literature and of the past as I am, allow me to include in this letter yet one more concept from the Olden Days, and that is the concept of the medieval Wheel of Fortune—not the game show of the same name, Bob, but the whole concept, which goes/went as follows: even though one day—today, for example—you may be at the top of your personal carriage wheel, as far away from the mud and stones and filth of the roadbed as it's possible to get, in just a little while that wheel will turn again, as your carriage, Bob, rolls forward, and you'll be back on the bottom, and then, if your carriage happens to park in that position, that's where you could be stuck for a really long time.

Truthfully, I'm not sure where this is going, but if you're interested, Mandy has called this letter, which I ran by her in draft form before I send/sent it, a "cry for help," and in fact she told me to stow it, although if you think she is about to run off and squeal to the cops I might remind you of the professional oath she and other such therapists must take regarding the privacy of all such patient/doctor communication.

I hope you are understanding me.

I really do.

Yours truly, The Wagonmaster
(formerly known as Dennis)

Wagonmaster, I asked myself, what kind of name is Wagonmaster?

I remembered vaguely an ancient television series about a man with the same name whose Sisyphean task it was to guide wagon trains across the Old West. Each show depicted some bogus human drama (almost always including loss of life), and I myself had watched a few episodes chiefly because it aired following the classic *Wilderness Camera*, a program that simply left a camera on a mountain top or alongside a river to record everything that passed before its lens for a month or two, then edited it down into an interesting and informative half hour. Sad to say, *Wilderness Camera* had long been disgorged from the fickle maw of television, while *Wagon Train*, with its ersatz sense of migration and fake human drama, turned up all too often on reruns.

"Wagonmaster," I repeated, and I resolved that from that time on, I would not let Dennis—or whatever his real name was—bother me, but instead would pour my every ounce of energy into perfecting the Communicator, because, ironically as it turned out, the Communicator was the very project that Bob himself had instructed me to complete as soon as possible.

15

And just in case anyone at all is listening, now I'm back!

I think that coming and going must be part of this place, because whatever lets me talk, or project, or broadcast—whatever it is—gets strong and then weaker, like radio waves when Yvonne, my mom, used to drive us into a tunnel while we were listening to her favorite station, AM 640, the Mellow Mist. Or maybe it's like an Internet wireless connection we get from the apartment next door to let us get the Internet, although I'm not supposed to tell anyone this is what we do. I mean I *wasn't* supposed to say that, but I don't think it still counts, what with everything that's happened.

Does it surprise you that my best friend here is Bob?

Well, actually, Bob is my only friend.

Yes, you are right! He's the exact same Bob who bit me, but you should know that when he did that bad thing, Bob was really sick with the same sickness he gave me. So Bob says that when he bit my arm—which wasn't even all that hard because he barely broke the skin—he'd been feeling sort of dizzy, like a person in the show on drugs that Officer Stephanie brought to school—and that he hadn't meant to hurt me at all. Bob said that he only wanted to send me the strongest possible signal to stay away from him for a while because right then he needed a little personal space, and, because he's a dog, that signal happened to be a bite. An overbite, I guess you could call it. For whatever it's worth, he says he's really sorry and he feels much better now.

"But, nevertheless, I was wrong to attack you," Bob adds.

"It's OK, boy," I tell him. "Don't forget I've had rabies, too, so I can understand it makes you cranky."

In any case, when I arrived there was nobody, as I said, except Bob, who I could see, and was waiting, wagging his tail, trying the very best a dog could to make me feel less scared, but I have to say I *was* scared, because it was all so strange.

And still is.

"Bob," I say, "don't worry so much. I forgive you, and in a way, we are like blood brothers now. And, really, your wagging helped a lot, too."

Bob continues to wag.

"But I miss my mom," I tell Bob. And he tells me about his owner, who, he says, was pretty much an asshole, which makes me laugh coming from a dog, because sometimes my mom would say "asshole" when she was talking about my father, whom I never met. Even so, Bob says, he misses the man, because dogs have no choice but to be loyal forever, and so on and so forth.

"You understand that's the way I'm programmed," Bob says, and I'm not entirely sure Bob even knows what he means by that. Do dogs get a language upgrade, too? I'm guessing this is so because otherwise I shouldn't even be understanding him, right?

Bob hasn't seen any other humans, either, but supposedly there *are* other dogs here, he says. Well, not dogs, you know, but their presences, he calls them.

"What's a *presence*?" I ask him.

"It's an animal thing," he tells me. "There's no way you can get it. Sorry."

There are a few cat presences, too, Bob claims, which makes sense because I know that a lot of them are put to death in animal shelters. Sometimes when I was bad my mom used to say that's where we would have to live—in a homeless shelter—so I had to behave, even though I don't think she really meant it.

These alleged presences don't talk to me, however, just Bob, and I can't see or hear *any* animals besides Bob: no dogs, no cats, no rabbits, cows, horses, wild animals, or birds of any kind.

On the other hand, it could be that everyone and everything in the whole world that ever died is here, for all I know, but out of all of them, Bob is the only one I can actually see. How come I can see Bob and nobody else, not even me?

Bob says it's because we have a bond through that disease, but I'm not sure.

What I am trying to say is that without Bob I would be completely alone, like sometimes when Yvonne has to be at work and she leaves me all by myself in our apartment.

I mean she *used* to leave me.

16

Sometimes a person can prepare for every eventuality, can put up screens, for example, to keep out mosquitoes, flies, moths, and bumblebees, and then, exactly when he thinks that he has covered all his bases, a hornet will sting him right in the middle of the forehead. This happened to me once several years ago, and I wound up having to spend practically an entire Sunday in the emergency room.

The day after I had gotten and read the semi-anonymous desperate letter, I inspected the Communicator, putting the helmet on and taking it off again a few times. It felt as if it had always been there. After that, I completed a daybed that was supposed to have been ready long ago. I'd told its owner I was having trouble getting the fabric, but, honestly, lately so much had been going on my heart wasn't in it. Bob's admonition not to let my business collapse beneath the sheer weight of my creative impulses was better advice than I had considered at the time. And then the doorbell rang.

I walked over to answer it. Maybe, I thought, Yvonne had decided that she was ready to accept some outside help in her grieving, and who better to provide that help, she would have concluded, than someone she'd known in the past, and wronged, but who never had uttered the slightest word of reproach, and instead had treated her and her daughter to multiple helpings of surprisingly tasty cake? How quickly things in life could change; no one knew that better than me.

"Don't worry, Yvonne," I would tell her, maybe rubbing her shoulders the way I used to—the way she taught me—to loosen her tense muscles. "Grief has its own timetable. Take as long as you need to complete your individualized healing curve, but just get better."

But upon opening the door, I saw, instead of Yvonne, a short, wide man with a head that looked as if long ago—possibly when he was a teenager and did the crazy things that teenagers do—he had put it between the jaws of a vice and then, either by accident or on purpose, tightened it. His hair was blond and curly; his eyes were small, the size and the blue of cheap jelly beans. He wore a Cleveland Indians baseball cap. His upper lip, long and droopy, sagged above an entrance to an oral cavity that looked as if it had been put together from leftover mouth parts. I could see a small, gold combination lock, the kind they make for suitcases, hanging from one pierced ear. It matched his right incisor, also gold. His forearm had been freshly tattooed with a single word: *BOB*. Each letter was a rattlesnake.

"You must be Dennis," I said.

For a minute the man looked angry, and then confused. He blinked and turned as if to go, then changed his mind.

"The Wagonmaster," I said. "Come in."

He stepped inside.

He was scary, and yet somehow beneath this menacing, even near-vicious-appearing exterior, there was also a shy, and conceivably even gentle, individual (how else could he have been so attached to a pet?) who was probably at that very moment hurting so deeply he just needed someone to whom he could express the full extent of his pain, a man for whom his former, written screed, as vicious as it was, was just not enough, and who longed for human sympathy.

It was weird how the grieving business had managed to knock at my door, even if it didn't turn out to be Yvonne.

"You're Bob's former owner," I said. "I got your note. I would have called you earlier but had no way of knowing who you were, let alone how to contact you. As you must remember, there was no phone number on Bob's collar, in fact there was no tag at all—not that I'm blaming you for that. Sometimes things like that happen even to the most devoted of pet owners. Would you care for a cup of tea and maybe a few cookies to go with it?"

He flexed his large biceps several times in thought. "Yes," Dennis said, "his former owner. And the little round tag with my phone number fell off a week or so earlier when Bob dove into a privet hedge after a ground squirrel.

He caught it, but I've been beating myself up ever since the accident. I don't suppose it would have stopped that car from hitting him, though."

"If it's any comfort, I'm sure it wouldn't have," I said.

Dennis fell heavily onto the same couch Dee Dee had once occupied, expanding and contracting the size of his body like an emotional concertina. "I *would* be happy to have some tea. With milk and sugar if you've got it."

"No problem," I said, and I went into the kitchen, where I heated some water and looked around for some easily concealable implement of self-defense. A knife seemed too aggressive and might actually provoke the Wagonmaster. Who knew what hidden psychotic triggers may have been implanted in his unconscious? A fork was too imperfect a weapon, and a spoon was just plain ludicrous, so, in the end, I settled on a triangular pie server, which had the advantage at least of looking more dangerous than it probably was. I laid it on the tray next to the cookies, should I find it necessary to defend myself. It looked less out of place than I would have guessed.

Back in the living room, over tea (Dennis took three lumps of sugar and a dash of milk), I explained to him how I had been busy at work the day of Bob's demise, heard the thump, and hurried outside to see Bob making his unsteady way toward me. As I spoke, Dennis's face was a movie screen of emotion, going from previews, to the opening scenes, to the dénouement, and, finally, to the credits in about a minute. "I don't think he felt any pain," I said. Then I explained my dilemma regarding the disposal of Bob's body, a problem Dennis seemed to appreciate. "If you'd like to take a stroll with me into the backyard," I told him, "I can show you where Bob is resting at this very moment."

Dennis ate another chocolate chip cookie, downed the last of his tea, and blinked. "I'd like that," he said.

I wondered if Dennis was one of those multiple-personality types I sometimes read about who are prone to sudden mood swings. At the moment, he seemed pretty much under control, except, of course, it's exactly when those types lull you into a false sense of security that they are most dangerous.

We walked outside and I pointed to the rosebush. Aphids were eating its leaves and it was going to need a good spraying one of these days. "See," I said, pointing to the marker.

Dennis's eyes filled with tiny tears. "That's a beautiful sign," he said. "Did you go out and have it made especially for Bob?"

"As a matter of fact, I painted it myself," I told him.

A look came over Dennis's face, as if he were trying to solve some difficult math problem. He walked over to the hawthorn bush in the corner of the yard, snapped off a couple of branches in an absentminded fashion, and walked back toward me. Involuntarily, my hand drifted over to the pie server, which I had tucked into my waistband.

Dennis tossed the hawthorn branches onto the grass and ground them with his feet for a while. "I loved that dog," he said. "I got him from the shelter as a pup. You know the shelter?"

"Yes," I said, and for a moment I had a vision of Marlene taking off her Animal Technician One outfit after a day at work.

Dennis looked at me again as if he had decided something important. "Listen," he said, "Would you mind leaving me alone here for a few minutes—you know—so I can breathe in the roses . . . and the rest?"

"Sure," I said. I went back inside and ran my finger over the edge of the server; it was surprisingly well honed. By the time I'd finished rinsing the teacups, Dennis was standing next to me. "So," he said, and he put his arm around my shoulders, keeping it there for just a bit too long to be comfortable. "I guess I might have misjudged you. I apologize. I'll sleep better, knowing about Bob, and about you too, Bob."

We walked through the living room to the front door, and Dennis took one last look around. "Say," he said, "I know it's not my business, but what's all that under the blue tarp?"

"Oh," I said, "that. Electronic stuff. Just a lot of equipment I'm fooling with. You take care of yourself, OK?"

"I will," Dennis said. "And you—you watch out for speeding cars."

And Dennis left, feeling slightly better, I hoped. Still, my guess was that I hadn't seen the last of the man.

17

FIRES STILL BLAZE

The criminal (or criminals) who is thought to be responsible for at least 14 trash and other fires still remains at large. "I am confident we will track him down any day now," St. Nils Police Chief Russell Wilson was quoted as saying. "Good police work always pays off in the end, even if it takes a little extra time."

Others are not so sure. Angus McReedy, president of the Eighth Street Mall Merchants Association, states that unless something is done quickly, "this situation is a tragedy waiting to happen." Many of his fellow merchants agree and say that while they have faith in the police force, if nothing is solved soon they "may have to take matters into their own hands." When asked what that would entail, they refused to elaborate.

18

Here's what I've been thinking: I've been thinking that because when you're dead you don't take up any space (duh . . .), where I'm talking from could be anywhere at all. In other words, heaven could be in the sky (why not?), or underground, or even in somebody's garage, or on the head of a pin—a straight one, not a safety one. Not only that, there could be a whole lot of heavens. There's no reason at all to have just one; they could be stacked up, like storage units, anywhere, maybe even on top of each other, a jillion at a time.

Does any of this help get me out of here?

Well, no. But it gives me hope, because it means that wherever I am at the moment, I may not actually be as far away from my mom as I was afraid of being. For that matter, I could already be in our apartment—maybe in her bread box or in that place under the toaster that catches the crumbs, though I wouldn't like to be there at all; I saw it open once and it was a place way too sad and creepy to stay inside for long, even if it *would be* close to Yvonne.

And one more thing, though you probably already have guessed it: there is absolutely nothing to do here except talk to Bob, whose main subject seems to be that he still feels bad for biting me in the first place, which *is* kind of sweet, because I can completely understand the fact that he couldn't help it, but I'm also getting a little tired of hearing him repeat the same thing over and over. So there's that, and then in between the times he's apologizing, he'll just look at me and wag his tail to show he wants me to throw a ball for him.

Not a *ball*, exactly. More like the *concept* of a ball.

And then he finds it.

I mean, the concept.

Then sometimes when I refuse to throw it for him, Bob just sits and looks at me and howls.

What?

Oh, OK, Bob. Hello. Yes, I'll throw the ball. Ready . . . set . . . *Go get it, boy.*

Then he's gone a long time—a really long time—and when he returns he's got "nothing" in his mouth, not even the concept of a ball.

Like when I used to ask my mom what happened to my dad. "You don't need to know," she'd say. "All you need to know is that you had one."

And I would think: *Thanks for nothing.*

19

I had just picked up the yellow tennis ball I found in my backyard and was throwing it over the fence into Farley's yard, where it probably belonged, when my mind was flooded with memories of Yvonne: Yvonne sitting at her usual table in the library of the institute, chewing on the stub of a yellow pencil, her eyes closed as she tried to memorize the muscles of the human back, shaking her head and slapping herself on her hand, and making little moaning sounds every time she got one wrong; Yvonne in her two-piece swimsuit with a pattern of black and yellow flowers as she swam laps at the institute's smallish swimming pool, her tan, slim legs kicking behind her in either the flutter kick or the frog kick, depending on which stroke she had chosen that day, a pair of swim goggles with weird yellow lenses strapped tightly to her head as she sucked water into her mouth—the same water that had already been in and out of the mouths of all the others who were swimming laps along with her—and then spit it back into the pool in which all the swimmers, Yvonne included, had to stop every three or four strokes and turn around again because the pool was so small.

Then I pictured Yvonne sitting across from me at one of the tables of the Snack Shack, licking her index finger after she had just stuck it into a bowl of organic split pea soup to test the soup's temperature as a few croutons floated on its quiet, green surface; or Yvonne crawling in through the open window of my dorm room after hours so I could give her a back massage, lying on her stomach on my bed, beneath the poster of The Jackson Five, the skin closest to the hair by the nape of her neck slightly whiter than the rest of her skin, her blouse first having been removed so it wouldn't get wrinkled, her bra removed as well, the marks of its straps still visible, her shoulder blades rising in two gentle waves like two sleeping children, twins, either two girls or two boys, about three to four years old, who had fallen asleep together on the floor of their playroom surrounded by all manner of discarded toys, the light of the afternoon sun soft and golden. Then again, there was Yvonne, still in my room, but now sitting on my back, usually having put her bra back on, but sometimes not, her lovely pelvis resting just at the base of my spine, leaning forward, her firm hands kneading my shoulders, her lips close to my right ear and whispering, "You're so tense, Bob. You need to loosen up."

I thought about Yvonne on a bench beneath the institute's single elm, reading her poems out loud to me, the lined pages of her yellow legal pad fluttering softly in the wind as her words mixed with the sounds of birds, the murmurs of fellow students talking, and the clunk of pots and pans from the Snack Shack, which was situated practically on top of the elm. Every so often, I would offer her a grammatical suggestion, but mostly I just told her to trust her talent, because when she did, it always turned out wonderfully, such as the day when she asked me if I could think of a rhyme for *botulism* (in those days she was writing rhyming poetry), and I told her to trust her talent, and she did and came up with *Catholicism*. I remembered Yvonne wearing yellow shorts, watching me as I pumped up the tire of her bicycle, which had mysteriously gone flat. I remembered Yvonne boarding buses when the two of us would take a trip into the city for a movie and how, for one reason or another, even knowing ahead of time that she was going to be taking a bus, Yvonne would never have enough or the exact change and would always have to borrow some from me, which was all right because, having anticipated this, I used to carry around extra dimes and quarters.

And, of course, I remembered Yvonne walking away from me outside that classroom already full of other students waiting to learn how to speed up their reading using the Third Eye (I never did find out how), her white tennis shoes seeming to float above the scuffed, green vinyl tile of the hallway, her simple white and yellow sundress revealing just a hint of those shoulder blades I had once massaged so lovingly, the same dress hiding and yet revealing the graceful curves of her receding posterior, the backs of her calves, the backs of her arms, the back of her head, and how, once she had said good-bye, she never—to my relief and to my sorrow—ever looked back, not even once.

I heard the tennis ball bounce into Farley's yard—once, twice—and then hit something that made a tiny clunk. And finally stop.

20

SCENE: Someone, possibly a child, is watching a television set. He (she?) is sitting deep in a sofa, so all we can see is the back of a small head, fixed on the program he or she is watching, which is *Tiny Alley*. There are other things in the room, but to the child, the only thing that counts is the screen of the television set, even smeared with various foods as it is.

> FRANKIE CHIPMUNK: Today on *Tiny Alley*, we have a special guest, and his name is Bob.

BOB: Hello, Frankie Chipmunk. It's nice to meet you.

AUNTIE JUNE: Hello, Bob.

BOB: Hello, Auntie June. It's nice to meet you, too.

FRANKIE CHIPMUNK: And what has Bob come to tell us about today, Auntie June?

AUNTIE JUNE: Bob's going to tell us about his business, which is . . . (she holds out a microphone to Bob)

BOB: Reupholstering furniture.

All the animals in the background cheer, and Reckless Rabbit falls out of his chair onto the floor.

RECKLESS RABBIT: Ouch! Bad chair!

BOB: Wait a minute, Reckless Rabbit. Don't be so reckless. That may not be a bad chair after all.

Confusion and excitement are shown by the other animals, and by Auntie June as well.

BOB: All your chair may need is reupholstering.

We can replace the fabric that is on there now
with another one that isn't so slippery.

MISTER POSSUM: Wait a minute, Bob. What
is reupholstering? I never heard of that, and
before we try out anything that is new, we
should first have a good idea of what it is, and,
second, if it's safe. Don't you agree?

BOB: Yes, I do. Reupholstering is when you take
off whatever covering is already on a chair that
you don't like and replace it with some kind of
fabric you do like, and it's very safe.

ANIMALS AND AUNTIE JUNE: Hooray!

Reckless Rabbit knocks Frankie Chipmunk off his chair
and climbs on it to take his place.

RECKLESS RABBIT: You mean safe like this?

Boos from the other animals.

AUNTIE JUNE: No, Reckless Rabbit. That's not
what Bob means. You give Frankie Chipmunk
back his chair right now.

Reckless Rabbit gets down from the chair and sulks in a
corner.

BOB: Don't worry, Reckless Rabbit, you'll soon have your old chair back, and it will be better than ever.

AUNTIE JUNE: Let's all watch and see how Bob does it.

They all watch as Bob produces a razor-knife from under his shirt and slices off the old vinyl from the chair.

BOB: And now for some ultrasuede, guaranteed one hundred percent not to be made out of animals like you.

The animals applaud.

Bob takes some precut pieces and drapes them over the old frame. He staples them in place with a staple gun that Auntie June hands him. Then he takes a decorative ribbon and glues it over the staples.

BOB: That's it. We're all finished. Do you want to try it out, Reckless Rabbit?

Reckless Rabbit tiptoes up, as if he's afraid of the new-looking chair, and sits down carefully. He smiles, then springs out of the chair and points to it.

RECKLESS RABBIT: A lump! There's a lump in my chair that wasn't there before.

BOB: Why don't you let me take a look?

Bob rips out one side of the fabric covering the seat and reaches beneath it. He feels around for a moment and then pulls out a yellow tennis ball.

BOB: Hey! How did this get there? Frankie . . . ?

Frankie laughs to show that he had slipped it there as a joke while Bob's back was turned.

21

Talk about dummies leading dummies, by which I mean: I'm still here, along with Bob.

Woof to you, Bob.

Not that this is a truly bad place. Truly bad places are places such as the insides of dark closets, and hospitals, and underneath toasters, I guess. But this place, even though not truly bad, still is plenty scary.

I know, I said that.

Because this place is not a *place* like the kind you think of when you think of a place as somewhere like St. Nils, which is where I'm from, a place where you can walk to the store and have an ice cream and then come home again. It's more of a place like when my mom says, "This music puts me in a good place."

It was Bob's wagging that first gave me this idea: how his tail will go back and forth, but never really move, if you know what I mean. Or better than a tail, this place is more like an endless loop, not of events that have a beginning and an end, or even of the same TV show playing over and over, because that would still be in a kind of time, but this place is more like lots of different TV shows squished together—cartoons, and *Tiny Alley*, and *Survivor Man*, and *Zoo Brothers*, and news shows—with my memories mixed in, too, so while nothing here is new, exactly, it's not the same as it used to be, either. And the result is that although I'm able to think of as many things as I want to (and no one here ever stops me from thinking), I find myself thinking the same things over and over.

In other words, I guess this place is more like the mind of a person who's worrying—not in a bad way, like my mother, Yvonne, does, exactly, but in the sense of thinking about a problem and never actually doing anything about it. Because in order for me in this case to actually do anything—to go anywhere—I'd have to jump to some other consciousness— Bob's mind, for example—like in hopscotch. And Bob is on an entirely different loop, I'm pretty sure—a Bob loop, which could be even scarier than the one I'm in, if you know what I mean. My own loop goes something like this:

I   WANT   TO   LEAVE   I

WANT   TO   LEAVE   I   WANT

TO   LEAVE   I   WANT   TO

GO   HOME   AGAIN   I   WANT

MY   MOTHER   I   WANT   MY

MOTHER   I   WANT   MY   MOTHER

I   WANT   MY   MOTHER   BUT

I'D   SETTLE   FOR   ANYBODY   AT

ALL   OR   EVEN   A   LIVE

DOG

(No offense, Bob.)

Really.

22

I spent the night fooling with the Communicator, which was still making that irritating howling noise, and then, after drinking a glass of milk with a couple of raw eggs, I sat down at the kitchen table to stare out at my backyard. This staring-at-the-backyard-thing was getting to be a habit. There, next to the rosebush, was the same yellow tennis ball I had tossed back into Farley's yard the night before, or, at least, *a* tennis ball—I hadn't been paying enough attention at the time to notice the brand, and, anyway, it had been dark. Next to the ball was another object, only slightly larger, that I couldn't quite make out.

Was Farley sending me a message to show his complete lack of respect toward me? It certainly seemed so. I went outside. The object next to the ball was an empty can of black pitted olives, extra large, with a napkin stuffed inside. I picked up the ball and pushed it, or as much as would fit, into the olive can on top of the napkin, and tossed the can over the fence back into his yard. The man was just going to have to learn the hard way that I was not a person to be treated in this manner. Then I returned to the kitchen, where I found a bag of coffee grounds I'd been saving to spread around the base of the rosebush until Bob had arrived to save me the trouble. To that I added some potato peels for good measure, took it outside, and heaved the bag over the fence into Farley's yard to join the can.

Indoors again, I resumed my experiments with the Communicator. I replaced the batteries and jiggled the dials to be sure they were working, but all I could hear was that strange howling noise, or whining, or whatever anyone wanted to call it. Did the howl exist only in my head, or was it the result of some flaw in the circuitry? Unfortunately, like Marconi's early experiments, I had nothing to compare it to. But then, when I considered how far Marconi's wireless had come from the days when the high winds kept blowing his transmission tower down to now, with satellites in space, it occurred to me that one day in the future there might even be something like a Terminal Wave Television Network, and I would be at its head. I'd be rich.

For lunch, I went back to the kitchen to heat a can of mushroom soup and make some toast and another omelet and took them on a tray back to the bench to continue my work on the Communicator, making sure no crumbs came near the sensitive mechanism. When, about an hour later, I looked outside at the rosebush, there was a brand-new mound of garbage next to it. I walked out into the yard to inspect it more closely. The rosebush itself wasn't damaged, though several pieces of trash were stuck in some thorny branches, and Bob's headstone was completely buried by the stuff. If Dennis saw it, there was no telling what he might do.

I found a brown plastic garbage bag under the kitchen sink and took it outside to hold the trash. In addition to the tennis ball, the olive can, the napkin, coffee grounds, and potato peels, there were several empty liquor bottles (not a surprise, when I thought about it), two uncooked chicken backs beginning to spoil, a few days' worth of newspapers, several offers for credit cards, the top of a pineapple, a blue dress sock, an orange juice container, and a milk carton. I shoveled all of the above into the bag, adding a melon rind, a can of bacon fat, some long-ago mildewed pillow stuffing I'd been meaning to dispose of for the past few months, and another orange juice carton, along with several egg shells. "No time like the present, neighbor," I said beneath my breath, and heaved the contents of the garbage bag over the fence into Farley's yard.

Back inside, I found the camera I kept in my bedroom dresser and pulled a chair to the window to watch the proceedings. If Farley dared to strike again, I would take his picture and—seeing as I now had a contact in the police department—show it to Steadman. Either way, Farley had to be stopped. Maybe he'd wind up spending time in jail, or maybe he'd be let off with just a stern reprimand by the judge, but whatever happened, it would teach him to mess with me.

I pulled a copy of *The Fountainhead* off the bookshelf and began to read it while I waited for my neighbor's next move. The book was getting interesting. There was something about its hero, an architect named Howard, that reminded me of Howard Bonano. Maybe it was both men's refusal to compromise their vision that they had in common. It wasn't anything physical, for sure, and the architect didn't have that streak of white hair that Bonano did. Farley, apparently warned-off through some animal-like third sense, never appeared.

Then the phone in the living room rang, so I put the book down and walked to answer it. Maybe it was Yvonne, I thought, wanting to stop by and work on her grieving. "Don't worry, you've called the right person," I practiced saying as I walked to pick it up. "You can take all the time you need to grieve; grief is one of my favorite emotions, and, believe me, if you think a chat would help it along, I would love to have one."

"Hello," I said.

The line was silent.

"Hello?"

I couldn't even hear any heavy breathing.

"Hello?"

Nothing.

"Well, good-bye, then," I said.

I walked back outside to discover that Farley had used his cheap ruse of a fake phone call so he could dump back into my yard everything in the last pile of trash, plus a few other things, notably about a dozen empty ramen packages (no wonder he was crazed, living off that stuff) and what looked to be about twenty pounds of used cat litter. I admit, if I'd known earlier that the man was capable of loving another thing, even a cat, I might have given him the benefit of the doubt. Now, however, the time for forgiveness had passed.

I thought the situation over. Clearly, my great advantage was that while I worked mostly at home, and thus could pretty much keep guard over my own backyard, Farley actually had to leave his premises from time to time to go to work. Who would employ a person such as him, I wondered, but his earlier trick with the phone, far from angering me, had given me a good idea.

I found a trash barrel and went straight to a nasty stack of rotting leather I'd been keeping in the garage, hoping its smell, that of a dead thing, would diminish sufficiently for me to get close enough to throw it into the rubbish on trash pickup day, but it had only gotten worse. I held my breath as I heaved it into the barrel. Then I found a few other choice items and threw them in on top of it, along with everything Farley had dumped earlier.

Next, I dragged the heavy barrel alongside the fence in preparation for the second part of my plan.

Accordingly, I waited a few hours, to give Farley a chance to leave his house. Then I snuck up to Farley's big front door and, after banging hard on the brass knocker, I ran around to the side of his house, where he wouldn't be able to see me. If I heard the door open, I would go home, wait a bit, and try again later. If the man didn't answer the knock, I'd know he was gone, so I'd just return home and throw the whole mess back over the fence again—into the yard of the person who had started this whole ridiculous competition.

As luck would have it, at about four o'clock on that particular afternoon, Farley appeared to be away at work.

23

So here's the thing: I am sitting/standing/floating/something around when I think, OK, Dee Dee, in this place where you now find yourself, what do you actually have power over? And quick as a wink the answer comes back: your thoughts. Then I remember something my mother told me once, which was, "If you have lemons, make lemonade." She told me this once when I told her I wished I had a father like all the other kids at school, but what she meant I don't know.

What can I do with thoughts? I ask myself. Then I remember something else. Namely, that my mother—whose name I've already said about a million times is Yvonne, in case you should ever meet her—used to read me stories before I went to sleep each night, and what was great was that they all went somewhere. For example, *Goodnight Moon* started with the bunny awake and ended with the bunny sleeping, even though it stays in the same room the whole time. But then in another book called *Runaway Bunny*, this same bunny, or one similar to it, attempts to escape its mother. But no matter where the bunny goes, the bunny's mother follows and the bunny goes all over the place until finally the mother catches her bunny child, though that's really a baby book.

And, yes, I know I'm talking about a bunny who wants to get away from her mother, when all I want is the opposite. And if by any chance you are listening and do meet my mother, please tell her I love her a lot and still miss her.

If she could only find me.

"Stop woolgathering, Dee Dee," as my mother used to say.

Naturally, all this makes me think.

Dee Dee, I say to myself: time is motion, and if there is no time then nothing can move.

Isn't that what you just said?

(Dee Dee, you aren't helping here.)

But hold it, everybody. (I know, I know!) *This answer just in!* If I can tell a story, then that story has to have a beginning, a middle, and an end, correct? Which must mean that as long as *something* (my brain?) is moving down the line of words that I'm about to say—or tell, I suppose—into the air, then there *has* to be time of *some* kind, and—*ta da!*—if there's any time at all, even if it's only in words, then maybe I can use the story to create the motion that will move me out of here.

THIS IS IMPORTANT, EVERYBODY!

And I mean move *me*, the actual Dee Dee I am, and not just my thoughts, although honestly I would have to say *that* person who is me at this moment is a little hard to describe.

It's true I can't prove for certain that this escape theory has ever worked for anyone.

Unless everyone has escaped already and it's only me who's left behind.

But anyway, *if* I'm getting these words to you (and yes, this is a big *if*), they must be traveling somewhere. And traveling means a path that they have to travel along to get there, doesn't it?

And if this storytelling part is going to work, what story should I tell? I ask this because, honestly, to tell a story about Yvonne would make me much, much too sad. On the other hand, Bob here wants it to be about him, but, frankly, Bob, I'm not sure the story of a dog is enough to get me personally out of anywhere, though, yes, I know it might make you feel better, and also I could use you (I'm talking to Bob here, if you haven't guessed) as a test subject, and so on and so forth. The problem, Bob, being that by the time I knew if it worked or didn't, something very bad could happen to you, because this whole place is new to me and I'm not sure I know all the rules. And something bad could happen to me, too, but then at least you'll be safe, Bob.

Maybe.

Bob says I should write about what I know, but I don't think he means write exactly, because what would a dog know about writing?

So here goes:

Once upon a time there was a little girl named Dee Dee, and she had a mother she loved and who tried as best she could to take care of her daughter, but often her mother had to work late at the casino, where she served meals and cocktails, and although Dee Dee's mother told her that the casino was named after an ancient Indian tribe and claimed to be run by its descendants, it was really in the hands of a group of Mafia goons, who kept hitting on Dee Dee's mother as she served really expensive meals such as the ancient Indians never ate, because their meals were pretty much confined to fish and acorns. Plus, the mobsters left no tips. "But just you wait," Dee Dee's mother used to tell her. "One day our ship will come in."

I certainly hope this telling business works.

And soon.

24

So I continued to refine the workings of the Communicator, and while some things were getting better, such as my ability to turn corners without bumping into things, at the same time the business with that on-again, off-again howl was beginning to drive me crazy. I kept track of the times I heard it, the directions I was facing when it appeared, but could find no pattern that made any sense, and instead of diminishing with added layers of soundproofing, the sound actually grew louder. When I took the Communicator off, I couldn't hear the howling at all, but when I returned the helmet to my head, at least half the time the sound would return, like the high C in the background of Robert Schumann's finest music made possible by advanced syphilis.

Again, harkening to the example of Schumann, I even wondered if the sound might be coming from my own head, although, in general, I felt pretty healthy. On the other hand, spending my days and most of my nights trying to track down the source of that howl was starting to wear me down. Could the interference be as simple as Farley making popcorn in his microwave, or was it somehow more sinister? Suppose there were other undiscovered waves out in the universe more than the Terminal ones that were trying (or not) to reach us? And if there were, were those other waves our friends or our enemies?

I practiced letting the Communicator warm up and cool down. I switched it on and off, first slowly and then in rapid fashion. I put the helmet on and sat wearing it with my head between my knees. I stood up. I lay on my back. At times the sound was there, and at others it wasn't, but I could find no consistent action that caused it to stop or start. The next step, I reasoned, was to find a person who wasn't me to test the Communicator so I could at least eliminate the possibility that the sound was coming from my own head. It shouldn't be so very hard, but whom could I find that I could trust not to steal my idea?

Then it so happened that precisely as I was in the process of considering all of this, my camera close at hand while also keeping a sharp eye on my backyard in case I spotted Farley, the doorbell rang.

"Bob, my man," Dennis said. "I was in the neighborhood, so I thought I'd stop by to see how you're doing." He flicked the top of a cigarette lighter, an old-fashioned, silver Zippo, up and down. It made a threatening, hollow sound and I could see why he liked it.

I must have looked confused, because Dennis stopped clicking the lighter, though he still kept it in his large hand. His nails needed cutting, or cleaning, or both. "You said I could stop by anytime," he said. "Then Mandy told me I needed to reach out and touch someone before it was too late, but she didn't say too late for what or who I was supposed to be touching—though she did say that it wasn't her. So I thought, well, this is anytime, and then I thought of my friend Bob, and I want you to know it's getting easier to say that name, Bob, without feeling anger."

I didn't actually remember telling Dennis he could stop by at all, but he was looking much too unhinged to argue with.

"So, Bob," he said, "here I am, and, if you don't mind, I kind of need to spend a few more minutes alone in the backyard to communicate with Bob. I know he's not a person, but it seems like a place to start, and I'm thinking a talk with him will help me out right now—if you get my drift. Actually, Bob never said much while he was alive—mostly he just kind of whined when he wanted to go out—so in a way this isn't all that different."

Dennis did a little dance like Auntie June in a kids' show I watched once in a while called *Tiny Alley*. Both Auntie June and Dennis were rumpled, large, and probably under the influence of one illegal substance or another. I imagined Dennis and Bob taking long walks together in the evenings, Bob sniffing trees and chasing cats beneath parked cars, Dennis waving his fist at passing motorists and shouting random thoughts into the air. He didn't seem to be an individual who had a lot of inner resources to draw on.

I considered: if Dennis went into the backyard, he might notice the deteriorated condition of the rosebush and become more upset. There was still a bit of Farley's trash clinging to it, and although I could have removed it at any time, it gave me pleasure to look at it and to remember how I had been the victor in the battle of the trash. On the other hand, I had a feeling Dennis would not take no for an answer.

"Sure," I said. "Be my guest. I'll be inside working on a project in case you need anything."

Dennis walked heavily through the house and into the kitchen. He pushed aside the sliding door to the backyard and stood in front of the rosebush, breathing in, I supposed, the perfumed molecules of his old friend and thinking who-knows-what about the good times they'd had together. The rosebush, including trash, looked ragged after last week's storm, but it would survive. I watched through the kitchen window as every so often Dennis put his hand into his pants pocket, pulled out his lighter, and gave the lid a flip, sending some kind of signal down into the soil—a semaphore, or maybe even a greeting—to his old friend.

Twenty minutes later, Dennis was back inside. "You wouldn't happen to have some coffee?" he said. "Instant is OK, and you really should clean that stuff off the rosebush." He looked a touch calmer than when he had first arrived.

I boiled up some water and made him a cup. "I plan to get to it," I said.

He stirred in three teaspoons of sugar. "It's not so much that Bob died, you know," he said. "I mean, everything passes; I know more about that than most people, having lost both my parents at an early age and having been raised by strangers in one uncaring foster home after another. Did I mention that I got Bob from the pound? Though I have to admit it was Mandy who pointed out the connection. But the fact that I wasn't there with him at his last moment, and that it was a complete stranger, you, Bob, instead of me, hurt bad—in the past, I mean—not so much right now. You know, I forgot to ask: did he make any gesture when he died? I mean, like he was looking around for me or wishing I was there? It would be hard to know that he was, of course, but it would also be a comfort, if you get my drift."

"Kind of," I said. "Where do you live?"

Dennis pointed down the street.

"Well then, yes," I told him. "That's exactly the direction Bob kept looking toward at the end."

Dennis brightened up a bit. "I'm not surprised. I miss having seen that, but I'm glad that at least his last minutes weren't with some uncaring person who couldn't tell how special he was." Dennis blew on his coffee.

"They certainly weren't," I said. This was not the time to contradict him. Something about my description of Bob's last moments had returned Dennis's level of agitation to what it had been when he first arrived, and beyond. I could hear the click of his lighter's top opening and snapping shut faster and faster from beneath the table. The man was starting to make me nervous, and it seemed to me that it would be good if we moved away from this particular subject. I had an idea.

"Dennis," I said. "I know you're busy and upset and everything, but if you have a minute to spare, I have a favor I'd like to ask before you leave. You see, I'm working on this invention and I'm having a little trouble with it at the moment and I need someone to help me test it. I can't tell you what it's for right now, because that would spoil the test; the only thing you need to know is that if this gets off the ground it will be of enormous benefit to all mankind, both in the present and in the past—and to dogs, also, by the way."

Dennis looked puzzled but shrugged. "Sure. Why not? It's not going to hurt, is it? Because in the foster homes, they . . ." he trailed off.

"No," I said. "It's really just to check a noise I'm getting every time I put this over my head." I pulled away the blue tarp to reveal the Communicator, and Dennis gave a little gasp.

I explained: "When I wear it myself, I get this sort of high-pitched sound. It's not loud, and doesn't hurt, but it comes and goes, so it's important I figure out whether it's from inside my own head or from somewhere else. Do you mind?"

Dennis stared at the Communicator, and I must say that seeing it through his eyes, the Communicator did look somewhat sinister, roughly like one of those giant acorns that are a prominent part of the façade of the Chumash Indian Casino. But this one had been plastered over in egg cartons and bound in duct tape, transformed, in a way, into a work of art.

"Don't worry. It doesn't weigh that much."

Dennis looked from the Communicator to me and back again as if there might be a trick. "OK," he said, and gave a kind of grimace. "Sure. I'm not worried."

I told him that I was first going to put the headphones over his ears, and then place the helmet over those. He would tell me if he could hear anything with the microphone turned off, then I would switch it on and we'd try again. "It shouldn't take more than two or three minutes, max," I said.

Dennis held still and waited. 1) The headphones. 2) The helmet. 3) Turning the helmet around so he could look out of the slit. 4) The microphone, still silenced.

"Do you hear anything?" I asked and, when I got no answer, I was gratified to know he couldn't hear me. I quickly found a pad of paper and wrote my question. I held it up to the viewing port.

Dennis shook the acorn sideways, no.

I took the pad. "OK," I wrote. "I'm going to turn the microphone on now."

The acorn nodded.

I flipped the switch, but Dennis showed no reaction. I wrote, "Do you hear a high-pitched whine?"

The acorn shook no.

"Try aiming the microphone in different directions," I wrote.

Dennis began to turn slowly. Through the viewing slit I could see his eyes, which were, if anything, smaller and more tense than ever. Then the slit moved away, and I could see only the cartons and the duct tape at the helmet's back. They were holding up well, I was pleased to note.

All at once Dennis stopped cold, dropped the mike, and tore the Communicator off his head. It rolled into a corner where it rocked for a while before it stopped about three feet away from the headphones.

"What? What happened just then? Did you hear the howling?" I looked at the floor. The Communicator appeared to be undamaged, thank goodness.

Dennis seemed dazed.

I repeated my question. He blinked once slowly and then kept blinking. His face was contorted in a way it hadn't been even when he had come to see me on his first visit.

"The howling?" I asked.

Dennis shook himself, as if ridding himself of a bad dream. "Howling? I didn't hear no howling. Is this some kind of a dirty trick you have set up to make me feel bad, because if so . . ."

I looked at him. There had to be more, but I couldn't guess what. "What are you talking about?" I asked.

Dennis's eyes got red and his big hands squeezed into fists. "All I heard was an airplane, and then a baby crying, and then some guy's voice going on about running over a dog. Something about getting a dent taken out—and do you know what—he didn't even sound like he cared. The prick was laughing."

"Don't be rash," I said. "It probably wasn't Bob he was talking about. It was probably some other dog, maybe killed in the last day or two. I think that it would be a good idea if you brought this up as soon as you are able with Mandy."

"What is wrong with you?" he said. "You don't get the point at all, do you? It doesn't make a difference. Mandy's good with a lot of stuff—I'll give her that—but she has no idea about people who are really bad. This guy's type is all the same. I'm going to find him, whoever it is, and make him pay. You think it makes any difference whether this was the exact person who murdered Bob, or only someone similar to the person who killed him? Well, it doesn't; the principle's identical. This prick hit a dog and doesn't even care. What can you do with somebody like that? I'll tell you what you can do—you can make them really, seriously sorry."

25

This is getting bad.

Something *is* starting to feel different here, wherever "here" happens to be, but instead of a positive change, it's like I'm both shrinking and fading at the same time now, and I wonder if the story is causing it, even though I just got started. I think I have to keep on telling it, anyway, despite the fact that all the effort is making me very tired, and not just me, but Bob, too. I don't mean he looks smaller, or faded, or is panting more, or wagging less, or anything like that, though. Mostly, he doesn't want to play as much as he used to. Instead, Bob sits around howling, which of course would be annoying anywhere else, but here it seems more or less OK, and what actually is weird is that it even makes me feel sort of good, like the wind when you're sitting on top of a hill, or the background music in an elevator when you don't want to think about the fact that you're going up that elevator to see the doctor and you're probably going to get some shots. And so, you see, it's exactly the fact that it's *not* bothering me that makes it the scariest thing of all.

Time is motion and motion is time, right?

Bob—would you mind not howling for a minute? No, it doesn't bother me, but I'm trying to talk here.

Bob?

Hey, Bob, find the ball.

Or at least the concept.

Hooray, the concept of a ball made him stop howling—or maybe it's just the concept of howling, because things are confusing here.

Though I kind of like the howling, because it tells me I'm not alone.

I said that already, right?

And though when I tell Bob "look" I can't know exactly *what* it is that he's looking at, at least he's paying attention to *something*, which is the "something" that I'm about to throw, which Bob brings back to me and I throw again, etcetera. So this is progress, I think, though I'm not exactly sure how. Anyway, at least Bob's happy to be doing something. With "something."

That is, I *think* Bob is happy.

When he's fetching.

When he's not howling.

Would I have been pals with Bob in my last life?

By which I guess I mean: life, period.
Maybe.
I wish I knew if this story thing is working.

And this girl, Dee Dee, liked animals, because when she was home alone she watched a lot of nature shows—Tiny Alley, too. And one morning, when Dee Dee was getting ready to go to school, her mom had to run back inside because Dee Dee had forgotten her lunch, which was in her favorite dolphin lunch box, and while Dee Dee was outside waiting in front of the entrance to their duplex for her mom to come out again, next to one of the big flower pots full of geraniums, which smell funny when you squish their leaves, who should come wobbling up the walk but a big brown dog, although at that very moment the dog didn't look so nice as the other dogs she was friends with, and not even close to Princess, who was one hundred times nicer and belonged to her teacher, Miss Zachman, and when Miss Zachman brought her to class one day and let Dee Dee hold her, Princess licked her face, and it felt really good and warm, like Princess wanted more than anything to be her friend, and nobody else's.

26

Even though I wanted everything to be as perfect as possible before I tested the Communicator in public, I could feel it straining like an impatient teenager to get out and leave the safety of his home, to try his luck out in the larger world. "But, Dad," the Communicator seemed to be pleading with me, "I need to learn to live on my own. I'm not a child anymore. I need to learn for myself if there are places beyond this house I grew up in where I can get in touch with the dead on my own. Think about it, Dad," the Communicator continued. "Suppose the dead have been trying to contact the two of us all along, and you and I have simply been in the wrong place to hear them, though not through any fault of ours, and that it's just this house? Wouldn't you feel dumb if that turned out to be the case? I know I would. What do you say, Dad, we take a little walk? Come on . . ."

"I'm not your dad," I answered, but then I stopped. The Communicator had a point, and it had been my own in the first place. I had been cautious long enough. Once again, this was the moment, and this time I was going to seize it and run with it, even if I couldn't say to where, exactly. It had taken me a long time (quite a long time, actually) to reach this point, and now Yvonne was waiting—Dee Dee, too—and I had promises to keep.

I had promises to keep to Yvonne.

And promises to Bob, too.

But I couldn't be a Reckless Rabbit. I had no doubt that there were other inventors more technologically savvy than I, and once they got hold of the principles involved here, they might easily beat me to the punch securing a patent. Once I was sure the Communicator worked as it should, then I could lock up the rights, and only after those rights were one hundred percent tamperproof would I present my invention to the public. I wasn't exactly certain how I was going to handle the whole legal aspect, but there were plenty of ads on television offering to help novice inventors such as myself. It didn't seem all that difficult a problem to overcome, at least not compared to my current search for those elusive Terminal Waves.

So I waited until it was well after midnight and then I finally donned my fishing vest filled with dry-cell batteries, picked up the directional microphone, and lifted the helmet—which hadn't been damaged by Dennis throwing it off—onto my head to walk again through the night, this time hearing nothing at all as the helmet swallowed each clunk and squawk and squeak of the natural world into its vat of thus-far howl-less darkness. That part, at least, was working. I could feel the familiar crunch of leaves and twigs and snail shells beneath my feet but, with the microphone switched off, everything remained dead silent. Cars, their headlights burning into the dark like angry thoughts, appeared and disappeared again. With the headphones over my ears and the microphone shut off, I could no longer hear a thing but my breathing and the beating of my heart. Except for the fact that I *wasn't* dead, I might not even have been human, only a camera attached to the back of a grizzly bear as he grabbled salmon out of a river, ate ripe blackberries, and dug roots (I'd seen this once; it was on a fairly obscure nature program called *Along for the Ride*). Walking in this way was like a dream, but a dream completely without sound. In its place, however, was a heightened sense of touch, especially on the soles of my feet—a body part, now that I actually thought about it—often neglected in the distant world of dreams.

Walk, walk, walk, walk. I switched on the microphone and tried, in a methodical fashion, to see what was out there, moving out from my house in an ever-widening spiral, listening for the first faint flutters of Terminal Waves. Point the mike. Point the mike. Point the mike. Night birds, bats, the whir of what might have been a moth, far, far away, an airplane (obviously, I was pointing the mike into the sky), but other than those empty tokens of contact, nothing.

I walked more. A few times I noticed that passing cars would slow (in complete silence) to check me out. Once, a driver rolled his window down, his lips moving, his face a picture of confusion and suspicion, but I never heard a word.

For some reason, there were a lot more people out on the streets than there had been at the same hour the evening I had come upon Yvonne's apartment completely by chance. Then, turning a corner near an old brownstone apartment building, I heard a different kind of noise. I stopped; the sound disappeared, and then returned, a definite contact. I waited, turning slowly in all directions, trying to get a fix on it.

I was right. I *had* heard something, but what? Was it the howl again, or a siren, or possibly someone singing very high, practicing scales? I listened; it *was* the same howl I'd been hearing earlier, but I was no longer at home, and the howl was, for some reason, more faint. I shut the microphone off. The howl disappeared.

I turned the microphone back on and the howl returned, but sadder now, if that were possible, like the faintest wisp of smoke that comes from a forest fire in a remote area of the wilderness that has all but burned itself out, leaving behind hundreds of charred animal corpses, small and large, birds, too, which had tried to fly away but had been overcome by smoke, a scene that was vividly portrayed in the documentary *Fire: Friend or Foe?* The answer to which turned out to be the latter.

In any case, I *did* smell smoke, although I couldn't tell where it was coming from. Then a police car appeared in front of me, stopped, and the door on the driver's side silently opened.

Once again history repeated itself, and I saw the familiar figure of Steadman emerge and his lips begin to move.

I removed the Communicator from my head.

"Bob," Steadman possibly repeated, "is that you? What are you doing out at this time of night, and what is *that*?"

He pointed to the Communicator.

"Oh," I said, "you mean *this*? I just rigged up something to hear a little music as I was—you know—walking around. I'm still having some of that back trouble I mentioned earlier. Do you like French music? It just so happens I'm listening to a really nice version of *Carnival of the Animals* by Saint-Saëns, and I could let you have a listen—it's one of his best, believe me." Never had I prayed more fervently that someone who did not look a bit like a classical music lover was not a classical music lover.

Steadman appeared momentarily puzzled. "Well, I'm more partial to the sound of easy listening, myself." I exhaled. For a minute I thought we were about to begin a discussion of musical likes and dislikes, but then he said, "Before I leave you to that long-hair stuff, would you mind holding out your hands in front of you?"

"Why do you want me to do that?"

"It's simple," he said. "I just happened to be driving home from my shift—getting to keep my patrol car is one of the perks of the job—when I got a call from the dispatcher on the police radio that somebody is setting trash cans on fire. I was in the neighborhood, so I thought I'd check it out. There's been no real harm so far, but as sure as I've been a cop for over twenty years, let me offer a prediction: sooner or later there will be trouble. Mighty oaks from little acorns grow, and that whole business." He looked at the helmet as if he were trying to connect something, but couldn't think of what. "Now, Bob, hold out your hands, like I said; I want to check them for traces of burn residue. I enjoyed our chat the other night, by the way."

I held out my hands; Steadman studied them, sniffed a couple of times, and nodded his approval. "You're fine," he said, "but I wonder if you have a minute. There's something I'd like to ask you, and it's personal."

"Sure." I hoped it would be short.

Steadman looked at me. "The truth is I'm only a cop who's nearing retirement age, but the other night, trying to rid myself of some of the tensions that build up at work, I drove out to that Indian casino just outside town, where I met a young woman. We got to talking—she's one of the waitresses there—and though this is probably really premature, I felt a powerful connection, one that I haven't felt with anyone for years, not since Jeannie left me to live with a commodities broker. You don't mind if I talk about this stuff with you, do you? I need to tell someone, but I'm not sure I want it to get out at the station house quite yet, if you know what I mean. Besides, she says she knows you."

"Yvonne," I said.

"Well," Steadman continued, "this Yvonne is certainly a lovely person who's suffered a lot, and anyway, for a long time I've been thinking about quitting the force here in St. Nils and moving to Las Vegas, where I know a guy who says he can get me a good job as a security guard in one of the casinos. I've been around long enough to know I should probably think about this longer, but tell me as her friend: do you think Yvonne would laugh at me if I asked her to join me? I'm probably old enough to be her father, but on a happier note, with my security guard income, plus my retirement, I'm thinking that Yvonne—I love saying that name—wouldn't have to work—that is, unless she wanted to, being as she already has experience along the casino line of employment. Yvonne writes poetry—I guess you know that—and while I don't know much about that particular art form, I think she has real talent. Listen to this"—he reached into a pocket and unfolded a bar napkin with a picture of an unhappy fish being roasted on a stick over an open fire.

Lawless man of the law—
Who knows what greater law
Will come to tame him?

"That's pretty deep, no? I'm still trying to figure it out," Steadman said.

"Anyway, in Las Vegas, Yvonne could have the time to really work on her poems, and maybe publish a book of her own. You know, I've been thinking that with technology able to create smaller and smaller screens, plus cell phones and text messaging, poems could even be the wave of the future. Not that I'm a student of the media."

I wasn't a media expert myself, but, actually, it didn't sound like a bad idea.

"So what do you think?"

I thought of telling him that he didn't stand a chance—not only because of his age but also because once I reconnected Yvonne with Dee Dee, there was going to be no force on earth that could persuade her to leave me a second time.

"I don't know," I said. "But I do know what you are talking

about when you refer to her suffering. Yvonne deserves better than her present life and being alone, that's for sure."

"Thanks," he said, "that means a lot to me." And then the possibly soon-to-retire policeman disappeared once again into his police cruiser and drove off into the belly of the dark beast that was the city of St. Nils at night.

I checked my watch. So much for my first road test of the Communicator. Steadman's talk of Yvonne had rattled me. It was time to give up for the night, get some rest, and hope that things—including the business of Steadman and Yvonne—would be clearer in the morning. I began my slow walk home, returning the helmet to my head because, despite the handle I had glued there, it was easier to wear—if that was the word—than to tuck under an arm, and then I flipped on the microphone, just in case. After a block or two the howl started up again, this time a little louder, as if whatever had been making it, weary and tired as it must have been, had roused itself to make one final effort.

I passed an apartment building whose vacancy sign was faded and peeling, hanging from its wrought-iron holder by only a single hook. I walked by an all-night party where someone waved to me; I waved back and I kept on walking, accompanied by the howl at random intervals. Finally, just as I was passing Farley's house—its lights completely off—the howl stopped. But in that millisecond between the dog's—if it was a dog's—final sound and the silence that would engulf it, I could have sworn that I could hear someone say the words, "Help me."

I went to bed.

27

Dee Dee, slow down.

You have to capture your audience the way Mrs. Zachman did when she told your class the story of Midnight, the black cat who got lost in the city and found his way home again after many adventures, including one with a rooster, and everybody was quiet because they were listening so hard.

And speaking of listening, right now Bob is doing that howling thing again, though I can't say I ever actually remember Bob having stopped, even though I do believe at one point he went off to look for the concept of a ball? Plus, I said, "howling *again*," so that must mean *something*, right—you see what I mean about this place messing with my mind—but then, when I try to remember exactly when the previous howling stopped and the new one started, the answer stays out of reach.

Did I say I kind of like the howling?

I'm pretty sure I did.

OK: So once upon a time Bob wasn't howling, but now he might very well keep howling forever, because it may be Bob knows something I don't. Although to say "once upon a time" makes me really sad, because it reminds me of how my mother would tuck me into bed at night and I would ask her to tell me about my father, and she'd laugh and say, "Oh your father . . . you mean Mister Lie Still and Keep Your Eyes Shut No Matter What You May Think Is Going On," and then she'd stare off somewhere for a minute, and shake her head once or twice, as if she was seeing him and not seeing him at the same time. And after that she would look back at me and shake her head again and say, "Dee Dee, how could I have been so dumb?" And then she would say it again. "Dee Dee," she'd say, "how could I have been so dumb?"

So where did my father go? The most Yvonne would ever tell me was that he was in a safe place, and I shouldn't worry.

But I did.

I just thought of this: maybe I like Bob because we're both missing our father figures—even though I don't think Bob is about to find his way home all by himself the way Midnight did anytime soon.

Would Bob have liked Midnight if he had ever met him in real life?

Somehow I doubt it.

Scared scared scared scared scared.

Help me.

Once upon a time, a girl named Dee Dee and her mother went to the hospital, which was very bright and full of a lot of grown-ups who looked really sad, and a man was bleeding from one of his eyes, and after Dee Dee and her mother waited a long, long time, a nurse who smelled like peppermint came and washed Dee Dee's arm, even though her mom had already done that while they were still at home, and then put on some new medicine where the dog had bit her. Then the nurse wrapped it in white bandages and put three happy face stickers on it, but two of them fell off almost right away.

"Has your daughter had her tetanus shot?" the nurse asked, and Dee Dee was happy to hear her mother say yes, so she didn't need one. Then the nurse turned to Dee Dee and said to her, "You are a very brave little girl. I don't know that I've ever seen a braver one. Now, don't worry. Tomorrow you'll be back in school and everything will be fine."

So then on the way home Dee Dee asked her mom if she could have a pet, a kitty of her own, and her mother said that she would think about it.

28

Dear Asshole,

I'm writing this to tell you your daughter died. Not that you'll care, probably, you being such a completely selfish and manipulative individual the likes of which I have never seen other than embodied in you yourself, but despite the fact that you never lifted the smallest finger to help her even before your richly deserved legal troubles, I thought you should know anyway. I also thought it might interest you to know that had you and I still been together (a thought that pretty much fills me with revulsion, just in case you might think it doesn't), her fatal dog bite probably wouldn't have happened, seeing as when—overwhelmed as usual by a million things I had to do because, as you wouldn't have the least idea, it's not a walk in the park to raise a child all by yourself—I forgot to be sure she had her lunch box with her, and had you been there you might just possibly have looked up from reading one of those stupid books all about what you used to call "the hidden powers of the human mind"—*right*—and told me I was forgetting something, and even if you didn't get that far, then when I was standing outside and noticed that the lunch I packed for her was missing, I could have shouted and it's possible, though probably not likely, you might have gotten off your fat ass for once and tossed it out the door so that I wouldn't have had to leave your daughter alone for what couldn't have been more than thirty seconds. In other words, if I had been with her that morning, then the dog, which I never even saw until it sunk its teeth into her arm, couldn't have bit her, because if I'd been there I would have certainly put myself between her and it before allowing it to hurt her for a minute—not something that would ever occur to you—and even after that, if it did somehow manage to get past me and bite her and I *hadn't* been distracted by all those small day-to-day tasks that every single parent must face—making school lunches, arranging child care, putting together costumes for various dramatic productions—and even if I *had* noticed her short period of mental depression (and what child without a dad has not been a little blue from time to time, especially when her dad happens to be a complete and utter shithead), her restlessness (try *not* to apply that to an eight-year-old), her headaches (which could just as easily come from constipation, if you know kids, which you do not), her fever (the flu was going around), her feeling sick to her stomach (stomach flu or a plate of bad leftovers), her tiredness (too much television late at night while waiting for me to come home from work even though I used to tell her not to), her stiff muscles (extra innings of four square), she might have been OK.

Because it was only when it was far too late for anyone to help that I really began to notice your daughter's excess salivation, her dilated pupils, her unusual sensitivity to light, sounds, changes in temperature, and, of course, her sudden fear of water. And then, by the time I was able to take a few hours off from my job as a waitress (thanks for the nonexistent child support) to find a pediatrician and then scrape together enough money from tips (having no health insurance) for a doctor's visit and get around to setting up an appointment, the disease really was past the point of no return. *Thank you, health-care safety net*. As for you—there you were in prison, getting plenty of rest the whole time this was going on, plus three meals a day with free dental and medical. And thank *you*, Asshole. Her name was Dee Dee, in case you ever wondered.

Not, I repeat, that I could imagine ever being with you anyway after that "shut your eyes" crap and everything you did with those other women, too, that came out at the trial. So I'm guessing that your spiritual gig was good while it lasted but unless I'm amazingly mistaken, I'm also thinking maybe that line of yours about having "trust in the future" is not working out so well in prison.

Do I think you are capable of understanding any of this, or feeling the least little bit of remorse? The answer is no. And lest you have somehow failed to detect a certain undertone of anger to this note, let me add that I hope you spend the rest of your rotten life rotting away there, where you belong, thinking every minute of every day about the wonderful child you never got to know, who, ironically, would probably have adored you, because that's how little girls are toward their daddies, even though a creep like you, with your pathetically infantile and narcissistic personality, would probably have figured somehow that it was owed you anyway and figured out a way to screw that one up as well.

Whereas the only thing owed you is a cell. Oh—and I almost forgot, your health benefits.

Because, you see, I've become a lot wiser in all the years I had to cope with the results of your deception, and life has made me a better judge of character than I was back in the days of the Mind/Body Institute, now happily shut down by the state and turned into a home for retired accountants.

In other words, you can just stay right where you are, in cellblock whatever, playing chess with your fellow cons and pumping iron like I've seen in prison movies, because your once-so-helpless victim, Yvonne, is not a victim anymore. Yvonne has moved on. Yvonne has people at her work who admire her and praise her talents. Yvonne has numerous friends, one of them being a cop, so watch out if you are thinking of ever trying anything. It also happens that another friend of hers is a former student of yours who agrees with Yvonne that you were never anything but a big, overweight charlatan, and this man is a successful businessman in his own right and a gourmet cook as well.

It sounds too good to be true, it is possible you are thinking as you read this, because I seem to remember hearing that line before from you and, just in case you think I'm lying, I have enclosed my friend's business card inside this letter so you can ask him yourself whether what I'm saying is true. I'm sure he'd be only too happy to hear from you and tell you what he thinks of you, too. And don't worry; he has lots of cards.

And finally, because an ordinary letter like this can't begin to cover everything I feel about your being unfit for any appearance at all on the stage of life, I enclose a poem that perhaps expresses my feelings in a way even you can understand (I'll bet you didn't even know I wrote poems back when I was seeing you, so self-absorbed you were):

> When it comes to rotten
> What is more rotten
> Than a rotting piece of crap
> Left out on the sidewalk
> And covered with flies?
> Hello, Mister Bigshot—
> You know who you are.

If you are detecting anger here, you are right. I hope they keep you in prison for a million more years.

Sincerely, Yvonne

29

Yvonne, who is my mother, used to say I had a good imagination, and maybe I do, but now I can't seem to find Bob's ball, imaginary or not, and how can anyone lose something that's not real when they're in a place that's not a real place?

If I had a head, this would be giving me a headache.

Then the next morning, because her mother had some extra time before she went to work, she kept Dee Dee home from school and the two of them walked around, listening for barking dogs and knocking on doors, which was strange and sad, because nobody but nobody was at home except for an old lady who didn't even have dogs or even like them she said, because she loved, loved, loved cats, and she offered to show Dee Dee and her mom the cats, and her mom was going to say no, but Dee Dee wanted to look, and so they got to see them, and there were two, both of them really fat, and one was black, just like Midnight, and one was brown with long hair. And then they left the cats and the lady, and Dee Dee was starting to get tired, and her mom was, too, when they knocked on the door of this house that was a little scary looking, and after a while who should come to the door but a tall, skinny man who looked a lot like a capybara, which is a South American rodent, Dee Dee knew, because one came to her school once along with some other animals in a traveling petting zoo.

And even though Dee Dee wanted to go home, the man invited them in, and because Dee Dee's mom knew him from before Dee Dee was born, they sat on his couch while he went to get them some cake. "Did you ever know my father?" Dee Dee wanted to ask the man, whose name was Bob, but she didn't. Instead, while he was gone Dee Dee wrote her name on his couch with blue ink using a pen she found behind a cushion so he would know afterward not to mess with her mom or he would be sorry.

But in the end, it was Dee Dee who turned out to be sorry.

30

There's a scene in old detective movies that always makes me sad no matter how many times I watch it, and I bet you know exactly the one I mean. It's where the private eye, who is usually smoking a cigarette, stands outside somebody's office. His hat is pulled over his eyes, and he's listening hard to what the man or woman on the other side of the frosted glass office door is saying. Then he throws the cigarette down, steps on it, turns the knob, and enters. This scene, as you know, works best at night, and whenever I call it up from memory, the hall outside the door is dark, and the glass, lit from inside the office it protects, is white with an unearthly glow, while—and this is the best part—

printed on the glass is the bland and mysterious name of an insurance company, or import/export business, or even the name of the private eye's own detective agency. But the private eye is always outside, and inside, behind the door, it's always someone else who's warm and comfortable.

That was the way I felt when I learned that Steadman and Yvonne had been talking—Steadman making his so-called plans for the two of them behind the door, as I, the gumshoe in the hall, the guy who was supposed to have the answers, was left out in the cold with yesterday's newspapers, still rolled up and unread, lying at my feet.

Just happened to meet a waitress, I'll bet—but guess what? Unbeknown to Steadman, I had the Communicator in one hand as my other hand was on the doorknob; I was coming inside, my gat at the ready.

Frustratingly, a whole week went by with little to show for it as I became tangled again in the task of bringing dead furniture back to life. I had to make a living, after all, but in between the fabric and the nails, I did what I could: I put a fresh set of batteries into the Communicator and tied a cone made of stiff plastic around the microphone so it could better scoop up any stray Terminal Waves. Every so often, I'd put on the helmet and the headphones, flip the switch, and listen, just in case. Whatever it was I'd heard at the end of my last walk had given me hope that there were certain portals—places in the barrier, screen, or whatever it was, that separated the living and the dead—that were less dense than others—if that was the principle—and thus allowed voices from the other side to be heard more clearly. Exactly *what* these portals were or were not made of, I had no idea, but that knowledge really wasn't important at the moment. My latest hypothesis was that for it to work properly, the Communicator, as powerful as it was, needed to be placed right in front of one of these portals. The plastic cone would serve as a funnel, like the end of a stethoscope, for the Terminal Waves. Also, it occurred to me that maybe the waves weren't even in the known spectrum of sound, so I thought that later on I might try resetting the audiometer so it would receive only those sound waves either too high or too low to be detected by the human ear—the kinds dogs are supposed to be able to hear. How exactly I personally would be able to hear them I hadn't worked out, but maybe they could be slowed down or speeded up through the use of a tape recorder. I made a note that one of these days soon I should make a quick trip to Ed's Discount Electronics to pick one up, just in case.

So I had just got caught up with my work, and was in the process of picking up the helmet of the Communicator and laying it back down, trying to decide whether or not to take it out for another run to see if maybe I could spot a portal or two, when there was a knock at the front door. Why didn't I know the kind of people who called ahead?

It was Dennis, his hands shaking and his face knotting and unknotting. On one shoulder of his windbreaker was a piece of something that looked like raw liver.

"I'm sorry. I saw your light on and had to try. I called Mandy, but all I could get was her answering machine, which had a message that she was on vacation and would be back in a month, but I can't wait that long." He looked helpless and ready to explode at the same time. "It's about Bob."

I thought about telling him to go away. It didn't seem like a good idea, however, considering the look on his face, so I just slipped a Phillips screwdriver into my rear pocket and said, "Why don't you come into the kitchen. You can sit down while I make us some tea? What's that smell, by the way?"

Dennis stuck out his hands. "I don't know," he said. "Maybe lighter fluid. Can I use your bathroom?"

He stayed in the bathroom a long time, but when he emerged most of the petroleum odor had disappeared, leaving behind only a scent of singed hair mixed with body odor.

When the water had boiled I put in two bags of Happy Moments (it seemed no time to offer Dennis choices), found what was left of a package of vanilla crème wafers, put them on a plate, and sat down at the table. Dennis sat across from me. Little by little, his twitches began to subside and his breathing slowed to a shallow pant. Was he on any medication and, if so, why wasn't it working better?

Then words began to dribble out of his mouth, slowly at first, until his hand—the one not holding the teacup—began to rub the top of his curly blond head, as if the friction generated by this rubbing motion would somehow heat up the molecules inside his skull, forcing his words to move more and more quickly until they were eventually expelled from between his lips, one at a time. Whatever the process, it seemed to be working.

"Need . . . to . . . talk . . . to . . . Bob . . . again."

He put the cup down, and the handle snapped off.

On second thought, whatever was on his jacket wasn't liver.

On third thought, his face was still doing that scary knotting and unknotting thing.

"Why don't you just run back there and pay him another visit?" I said. "How long is it going to take?"

"Not long," Dennis grimaced. "This is important." He handed me the cup and pushed himself up from the table as he headed toward Bob's memorial. "I'm sorry about the handle."

While Dennis was out back, doing whatever it was he did with his former pet, I thought about a time in the future when I would no longer have to put up with these constant invasions of my privacy, and imagined what my kitchen would be like when Yvonne was here with me instead of a possibly dangerous psychopath. There was the same Formica-covered counter and the same light green wooden cabinets, but now there was also Yvonne, naked, except for a frilly apron, and standing in front of the cutting board. She was chopping chives, because even when she used to cook me meals at the institute, she complained that onions made her eyes tear up.

That night, we were having chicken livers with chives on brown rice, and though Yvonne had finally gotten me on a healthier diet, come to think of it, I wasn't sure how healthy chicken livers were.

I blinked.

My kitchen went back to the way it always was, but now I saw Yvonne in Las Vegas with Steadman. Steadman was quietly leaning against a fake-marble pillar, wearing a cheap tux with a lump on one side where his shoulder holster was hidden, keeping his eye on things from a corner of a large, garish room in a smoke-filled casino as Yvonne sat at a blackjack table, halfheartedly playing out her hand. In between draws, she was trying to compose a poem about the old friends she had left behind in St. Nils, but was obviously having trouble. Maybe moving here had been a big mistake, she was thinking. Yvonne coughed a little and tried to concentrate. All that secondhand smoke was starting to be a problem.

I blinked and Yvonne—thank God—had transported herself back into my kitchen, still clad only in that tiny apron, and was now sitting across from me at the table, writing some of her thoughts onto a yellow legal pad by means of a brand-new felt pen. "I don't know," she said, "the Poetry Society wants to give me another award this week, and they want me to write an acceptance poem, but I'm having trouble getting it right." I stood up to give her a kiss, but she waved me away.

"Wait, I think I've got it," and she quickly wrote a line or two. "Now," she said. "I need you to listen and then tell me what you think. You know how I depend on you, Bob."

"Well, OK," I said. "I'll try. But don't forget you're the one who's the poet. I'm only a really successful inventor."

I blinked.

Yvonne was gone again and in her place was Dennis, who looked calmer than before he went outside, it was true, but also scarier in a way.

"I recently got some important news," he said, "and I just needed Bob's input before I did anything about it." Whatever had been troubling Dennis seemed to have been resolved.

"Do you have any more of those cookies?" He stopped to inhale deeply, held his breath, then exhaled. "And what's with all the junk still hanging on the rosebush? I thought you said you were going to take care of it. It looks like crap, if you want my opinion."

"I'm afraid that was the last of the cookies. And don't worry; the trash is part of an ongoing situation that's being handled."

Out of nowhere, Dennis's face flared with rage and then settled again. "Well," he said. "Dig it: I'm *this* close to finding out who killed Bob." He snapped his lighter, which he had somehow produced without my noticing. "All I need is the bastard's name—but don't you worry—I'm on my way to getting it."

Then the rage swept over his face again.

"What were you asking Bob about?"

"Oh—that's simple. Whether or not he wants me to kill the guy or just hurt him real bad."

"And he said what?"

"Bob told me that we only go around this world one time, and life is as precious to a dog as to anyone. He said as soon as I find the bastard who did it I should make him pay big time. 'Waste the fucker,' Bob said, and when I explained to him there were serious penalties for injuring a human, he only gave me this sarcastic-sounding laugh. 'What about the penalties for taking the life of an innocent animal?' he said. And I felt bad then, because he was so right."

"But how did you find out this information in the first place? Who told you?"

"Well," Dennis said, "I was doing a little detective work, like I explained, and who should I run into but your next-door neighbor. He said his name is Farley, and it turns out that he saw the whole thing, including you dragging Bob into your backyard, so you're definitely in the clear, my friend. Anyway, Farley said that he had been a little under the weather that afternoon, so he'd called in sick and was waiting at the window for the drugstore to drop off a prescription for a painkiller he said he likes to take when he feels bad, and guess what he sees? What he sees is this, if you can believe it: he sees a cop car going around a corner, not particularly fast, but it looks as if the driver is distracted because he's got something like a cruller or a slice of pizza that he's eating, and here's the thing, when this asshole hits Bob, he doesn't even slow down. This bastard, who's paid with my taxes and is a public servant, actually hits my dog and doesn't even stop to see if he's OK. Oh, and Farley said something about having a surprise for you."

I couldn't help it. "You pay taxes?"

"Well, sales tax."

"And you don't know his name?"

"No, but how hard can it be to find out which policemen were on duty on the day Bob died, and then track the murdering prick down?"

"Do you really plan to kill him?"

"Are you deaf or something? But I wouldn't be spreading this around if you happen to be thinking that way."

Dennis looked warily at the Communicator beneath its blue tarp and flicked his lighter a couple of times in farewell. "Anyway, thanks," he said, and he reentered the night to do who knew what?

The front door closed. So Steadman was a dog murderer. I guessed I owed Farley more than I thought for that piece of information.

I sat down on the couch, and suddenly Yvonne, who must have been waiting for Dennis to leave, was back again, opposite me in the living room now, wearing only her apron, reading a book of her own poetry, which had been published by a major house—unusual, for sure—one of the few times that's ever happened. The book was bound in red leather and had a picture of a yellow coffin on the front. Yvonne's beautiful red lips moved ever so slowly in order to reabsorb the sounds of her once-active grief over Dee Dee. Should I interrupt her? Should I say, "Yvonne, excuse me for a moment, but I just thought of the time back when, before the two of us got back together, you were considering moving to Las Vegas with that poor old retired cop, Steadman. Remember him? Isn't that amazing?"

How would she take it? Would she break into tears because she had been so easily deceived when obviously a better future mate (me) had been waiting right alongside her? Would she be embarrassed by her poor judgment in those days? She didn't have to be, considering the terrible state she'd been in, but I didn't want to upset her, so I said nothing.

Then, to my surprise, Yvonne was turning to me. "Oh, Bob, reading over these poems I wrote back when I was still in the depths of my despair over the loss of Dee Dee makes me understand how far I've come since then, and how much of that is thanks to you, and to my daily chats with Dee Dee. She says hello, by the way, and hopes your back is OK. I can't believe I was about to go with that silly Steadman person to live in Las Vegas. You've given me a whole new life. But the truth is, Bob, I only considered Steadman—and then only for a moment—because I didn't dare hope . . . and by the way . . . I wonder if you can give

me a hand with this apron . . . it seems . . . to be coming
loose . . ."

I opened my eyes. I was alone once again on the couch
looking at the poster of those Roman roads, and at a trail
of mud across the floor that Dennis must have tracked
through the house from the backyard.

I decided that the best plan would be to say nothing at
all to Yvonne, to let nature take its course regarding the
matter of her and Steadman.

Instead, I would redouble my work on the Communicator.
Eventually, Dennis would settle down and get back to normal, whatever *that* might be. As for Yvonne, it would be
soon enough—poor thing—that she learned what sort of
person Steadman was.

And just for your information, between Dee Dee's death
and then, it *did* occur to me more than once that when
Yvonne asked me for the second time about the dog that bit
her daughter, I could have just handed Bob over.

That way everything that followed would have been
Yvonne's decision, though it probably would have turned
out exactly the same.

But it's a little-known fact that only one out of ten
people who are bitten by a rabid animal actually contract
the disease, while, on the other hand, a surprisingly high
proportion of those victims who receive the antidote suffer
serious, life-threatening complications.

31

FORMER INSTITUTE HEAD RELEASED

WESTON (AP) Howard Bonano, the former president of the Institute for Mind/Body Research was freed from state prison here today, being released, along with several fellow lawbreakers, due to judicial rulings concerning the overcrowded conditions at this and other prisons in the state. Bonano, 52, who, in the brief time he ran the now-discredited institute, became infamous for falsified research data, the embezzlement of over $200,000 in tuition fees, as well as multiple improper relations with students, told reporters in a hastily called news conference that he was filled with "remorse and hope" upon his release. "I'm sorry for all the trouble I caused so many decent people who put their trust in me," he said. "It will be the goal of the rest of my life to win it back." When asked about his immediate plans, Bonano said he "was in the center of a situation that was continuing to develop."

32

Is Bob feeling pain here?

Another great question I don't know the answer to. By which I mean that judging from the sound of Bob's voice, not only is his heart broken, but his vocal cords are also starting to give out, and that must hurt plenty. But then, how can you have a sore throat when there's no actual throat? I wonder if that means you get to miss having the actual pain.

And now I've just figured out something else about this place I call the Land of No Time, and it's not even the pain-or-no-pain business, but something completely different: namely, that I used to think this place was some kind of infinite, and it is, almost. But lately I've been thinking that if there's an infinite, there has to be a pre-infinite, which is where I think I am right now. So *if* I'm right, while on the one hand I'm close to disappearing from everything forever, on the other hand, I still have some time left, or some of *something*, before I get to the *real* thing—by which I mean the *real* infinite.

"Lately?" What am I saying?

Which is why (sorry to keep repeating this) I keep on wanting somebody—anybody—to hear me, despite the fact that I'm not such a baby as not to realize there must be thousands—hundreds of thousands—of others who must want exactly the same thing at this very moment: babies who died at birth crying to be picked up; teenagers killed in car crashes who, when they were still alive and doing normal, boring teenage things, wanted their lives to be something great and tragic, but now would be perfectly happy to call some friend and ask what the day's homework was; moms calling to get back to their kids; other kids like me, calling their moms, though from where I am I can't hear any kids, or anyone else, for that matter—and thank goodness for that—because if I could hear them, I'll bet their cries would make a roar of sadness and longing so loud it would be even louder than Niagara Falls, where Yvonne took me once when I was still little after making me promise not to get scared, in order, she said, to show me something that I would always remember, and I do: the giant sound of a giant sound, and a mist coming up from the bottom, which was kind of like the fog here and kind of not.

Maid of the Mist was the name of the boat we took together, my mom and me, and now I know that she was right: compared to this, the falls weren't even close to scary.

Then Dee Dee's head was hurting a lot, and she was aching all over, and she could see her mom was getting really worried, and there was a knock on the door and some men in white suits had come to give Dee Dee a ride to the hospital in a real ambulance, and they let her mom ride in back, even though they said that was usually against the rules.

"But for you, Dee Dee," they said, "we'll make an exception because you are such a brave little girl."

"You are the bravest girl of all," her mother said, "and I promise I will buy you a kitten when you come home. It will be your reward for being so brave."

But by then, it was too late for a kitten.

33

The following morning, I noticed that somehow or other, as distraught as he may have been the previous night, the Wagonmaster had still managed to carve something— what?—into my kitchen table. Instead of a single wagon wheel, he'd drawn three, each on top of the next:

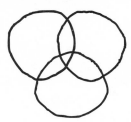

The man needed a few quick lessons in art school, that was for sure, but what was this trilogy of overlapping circles supposed to represent? Were they Dennis, Bob, and me? Yvonne, Steadman, and me? Yvonne, Dee Dee, and me? Yvonne, Howard Bonano, and me? The Past, the Present, and the Future? Maybe even Life, Death, and the Communicator. My head was starting to throb. It wasn't an especially good table, but his ruining it just to make some idiotic point made me angry, so in order to help me settle down I decided to take care of a tricky reupholstering job I'd been putting off for weeks.

It was an ancient love seat brought in by Randy, of Randy's Treasure Chest, a sort of old furniture and other things store. Randy had been a professor of art at the University of Art in St. Nils, where he had given up his tenure in order to make a bundle selling antiques. His basic strategy was to find pieces of furniture with sturdy frames but in need of new upholstery, buy them cheap, take them to me, and then resell them at a big profit. Why couldn't I have done the same? A good question. I might have, if I hadn't been so sidetracked by the Communicator.

The love seat, Randy told me, had belonged to an old Greek couple, and he had picked it up for next to nothing. Its fabric was threadbare and covered with stains of olive oil and what looked to be retsina. Randy had brought along with him a few yards of gold velour. "Have at it, Bob," he said. "Work your magic."

I quoted a price about double what the job was worth and he didn't blink an eye. "Tallyho," he said and left.

And there the love seat had sat for almost a month.

That morning, I was glad I had bid so high, because when I looked more closely, it appeared the job might take a lot of work. For one thing, the frame seemed to be all of a single piece—the back, and arms, and legs—at least I couldn't find where they'd been joined, and that sort of thing could be tricky.

Not only was the manner of construction unusual, but also, as ratty as it was, the fabric wasn't a print. It was a real tapestry, depicting the two halves of the human experience. Life was spread across the two back cushions, and Death lurked on the two cushions of the seat.

I'd never seen anything quite like it. The cushion on the left side of the backrest showed a baby being born, with the mother giving birth at home, in what I guessed was her own bedroom. There was a table next to her bed, a pitcher of water and a basin on it, and over to one side a doctor and midwife were engaged in some sort of argument, possibly over outstanding fees concerning the birth of the child who, very few moments earlier, had just emerged from its mother's body. The baby was a boy.

The scene on the cushion next to it, on the right, showed that same baby grown into a man and standing next to a barbeque grill, along with his children, a daughter of four or five, and a son, still a toddler. Apparently, the former baby had brought his whole family to a family reunion, because there were several other people present, all bearing a resemblance to him. His mother, still recognizable, but now grown old, was there, too, alive and well, along with several of his brothers and sisters, who must have been born after him, because they looked several years younger and were all really healthy looking, with big smiles on their faces. Not so the former baby, however, nor his wife, who was on the porch of the house in the background, lying in a kind of portable chaise-longue sort-of contraption that an illness had confined her to. She was obviously in pain. Meanwhile, the man, with a worried and stressful expression on his face, was holding a hot dog in one hand and a beer in the other, as if to ask how these two commonplace objects and others like them could possibly hold back the tide of human misery. A person couldn't help but wonder how things would turn out.

Sadly, the answer to that question was shown on the very first Death seat cushion on the left. It depicted a cemetery with many graves, and gathered around an open one was the same young boy and girl who had been shown with their dad at the barbeque in the previous scene. Their mother, still alive, was now confined to a motorized wheelchair. She had driven it up next to the grave and was holding out a bunch of flowers, getting ready, it looked like, to toss them in.

A person could easily guess what had happened: her husband, the very baby shown on the first cushion, having become despondent over his inability to provide for his loved ones, had locked himself into his garage and hooked the exhaust pipe of his car to a hose. Then he had secured the hose with duct tape to a car window that had been mostly rolled shut and sealed the crack between the top of the window and the door frame with the leftover tape. In the end, he had been found, too late, by a snooping neighbor who had been giving the man a hard time for not keeping his front lawn neatly cut, just possibly the straw that broke the camel's back. Such, the scene seemed to explain—even though no explanation was necessary—is life, and I wondered what Farley was plotting at that moment.

On the very last Death seat cushion, however, the picture was much more difficult to make out. Sadly, this particular cushion must have been the one chosen by a favorite dog or cat to curl up on, so not only was this one the most worn but also, out of all of them, the most stained. All I could discern at first was a large rectangle, white along the top, and blue on the bottom. Then, looking at it more closely, I saw windows, and while the upper ones seemed only gray squares, the lower windows were divided into little grids, like checkerboards. The place looked slightly familiar, but was it a house, or some kind of hotel, or maybe even a warehouse or a factory? It would be good to know, but though I stared for quite a while, in the end I gave up trying to remember where I had seen it.

The good news was that the fabric came off easily. Nor were there any problems with the frame. In the end, the whole job took less than half the time I had estimated and the gold velvet looked great. I left a message on Randy's answering machine telling him his couch was ready, and I was just hanging up the phone when I heard a knock at my door. Not Dennis again, I thought.

But when I opened the door, there was Yvonne, wearing a simple, yellow, sleeveless warm-up suit and a new pair of white tennis shoes. She had cut off most of her hair, which made her look younger, and she wore it in a simple, yet attractive wave, pinned at the sides by two child's butterfly clips. Was she coming to say good-bye, or had she turned the corner so that she was ready to begin the long hard climb up the stairs out of the basement of grief to the first floor of going on with life? I could feel my heart beat harder.

"Bob," she said, "do you have a minute? I'm sorry to be coming here without calling first, but I really need your advice. Not for me—I'm fine—well, not fine, exactly—you know—but it's for a friend of mine."

"Come in," I said. "I've been thinking about you. I'll heat up water for tea, and we can share some gingerbread I made a few days ago. Then you can tell me what's on your mind."

Yvonne nodded and we went inside.

The water heated quickly, and as we sat at the kitchen table, eating our gingerbread, I could sense something was wrong. "I know the crust is a little dry," I told her, "but I think some ice cream on top would help it out." I got up and found a carton of vanilla, which I scooped onto the plate in front of her.

Yvonne took a bite and smiled. "Thanks." She took a deep breath. "That does help, though I'm sure it would have been just fine without it," she said. "I don't know how to start, but let me try: Bob, I remember you were always pretty wise in the area of the mind, so I've come here today to ask for some advice—not for me, but for a friend. You see, my friend, she's had some trouble, that's for sure, and sometimes she doesn't even know how she's going to make it from one day to the next, plus she has financial pressures, too, like hospital bills. But here's the thing: in the depths of her difficulties, she's been offered what just might be a way out. Recently, she met a guy who seems steady and secure, maybe getting up in years, but though he hasn't known her long, he really seems to need her and he has a dependable retirement income, which he can supplement by working as a security guard. So now he's pressing her to make a decision to go away with him and to start her life all over again in another city, which my friend says isn't nearly as nice as St. Nils. But then, my friend also adds that as nice as St. Nils may be, right now she's isn't doing all that well here anyway."

A few gingerbread crumbs had collected on the edges of Yvonne's mouth, giving her a sort of little-girl quality. It would be easy, I told myself, to mislead such a person who had so much trust in me, in order to gratify my own selfish wishes. It was all I could do to try to be fair.

"That's a tough one," I said. "It's hard to judge what's best for a person. Sometimes, what's good for one person is bad for someone else, and what appears to be a safe choice is exactly the wrong one. This older guy, for example, he could have a stroke anytime, and then where would your friend be? She'd be spending her whole life working as an unpaid nurse, that's where. And even if that didn't happen, it's not a bit unusual for security guards to be shot and killed in the line of duty. I think there must be something about hanging around sipping coffee and doing nothing but gaining weight for long periods of time that makes it hard for a person to suddenly spring into action and defend himself against a prepared attacker when he least expects it. Basically, in those kinds of situations, if a bullet doesn't get the individual in question, then a coronary does.

"As for pensions, they dry up, and often what can seem like a safe bet suddenly isn't. And don't forget that by the time people get to be, say, ten or fifteen years older than we are, they have a history: ex-wives, ex-girlfriends, children, stepchildren, nieces, nephews, pets; there's no telling what your friend would be getting with this guy, who, it seems to me, even though he may appear to be in pretty good shape—possibly even better than a person like me, who manages to keep pretty active moving furniture and other things—has a definite potential to keel over on her at any minute."

Yvonne looked thoughtful. I could tell that she was listening hard to what I had to say.

I continued, "But just to be fair, you can tell your friend that with an older, semifailure kind of individual, she may be spared some of the disappointments that are well known to be part of the territory of dating younger men, things such as their leaving for weeks at a time on road trips with their buddies, and the discovery through cell phone records and the like of them having multiple sex partners. One woman will probably be more than enough for an old guy like that. Though, sometimes these older men are real chick magnets. I don't know what it is—thinning hair? bifocals? liver spots?—or maybe it's a combination of all the infirmities of old age: urinary problems, gout, nail fungus, Parkinson's, dementia, high blood pressure, deafness, joint problems, constipation, loss of muscle mass, late-onset diabetes, osteoporosis, tinnitus, retinal detachment, dropsy, cataracts, changes in the body's mechanism for regulating heat, thyroid dysfunction, gall and kidney stones, prostate enlargement, impotence, arrhythmia, and chronic cough, but there's *something* going on, that's for sure. If you want to know my opinion, it's nature's way of compensating one thing for another. Nature must have arranged it somehow that for each of these so-called maladies, there's some hormone, or maybe pheromone, released that has the effect of balancing things out. Taken together, you can imagine that the effect of such a dose packs quite a wallop for certain unsuspecting women, though I'm assuming his security guard job will be at a bank or auto parts warehouse in order to keep him away from eligible young girls, so things should be all right in that direction. At least your friend should feel good about that part."

"Hmm," Yvonne said. "What you say makes a good deal of sense, Bob. I'll think it over, that's for sure. And you're right; financial security is an issue. In my friend's case, for example, I only wish she felt a little less pressure from things like rent and everything. I happen to know her rent is due right now, and I'd hate to see her rush into a decision just because she's short a little cash. I'd give it to her myself, of course, but I'm sort of thin myself along those lines."

"Is that all that's bothering her?" I asked. "A little rent?"

"Well, probably not, considering everything, but, as I said, my friend does tell me that her current shaky financial situation is certainly making her feel the pressure to choose quickly."

"Just a minute," I said. I got up and went to my sock drawer, where I unrolled a pair of socks and took five one-hundred-dollar bills from them. It still left me with five more. I carried the stack out to Yvonne.

"Give these to your friend."

"I can't," Yvonne said. "But that is so nice of you."

"No, really," I told her.

"In that case," Yvonne said, "I'll only give it to her if she promises to pay you back the first chance she gets. I'm sure it won't be all that long. She's very nice, my friend is."

"Fair enough," I said, "but tell her not to worry. Tell her not to jump into anything too hastily that she may come to regret later."

"I promise," she said. "And by the way, did I ever tell you the true story of Dee Dee's father? He was an older man, himself, and you may be surprised to learn that you actually knew him."

"No," I said, "you certainly didn't."

"Well," Yvonne began, "the story starts back when you and I were students at the Institute for Mind/Body Research." And then she explained the real reason why she had chosen to break off our relationship, which, to my distress, involved the true story of Howard Bonano and the conception of Dee Dee and her death as well, sparing not the least unpleasant detail.

It was nearly dark by the time she finished talking.

34

So just as I'm getting a tiny bit used to not having a body—not *being* a body—*Wait!* Like those TV commercials say, there's more: because now *something is happening with my thoughts.* It's like I'm thinking and trying to tell a story, but at the same time there's an imaginary (what other kind would there be here?) trash container coming down over my head, and the story I'm trying to tell is getting hard to remember and making my thoughts invisible, too (OK, I know that thoughts are always invisible, but this is different), so that when I try to say what happened, before whatever-it-is can come out, instead I'm saying something more like "umm," or "hmm," or "huh."

I mean, I may be dead, like I have said earlier, but I'm not stupid.

Not yet.

But meanwhile, the rest of me (what me?) feels like I'm inside an ice cube—or actually *am* an ice cube—that's starting to melt, and though what's left is still me, somehow there's less of me than I remember.

I can't tell if the same thing is happening to Bob or not. I mean, he's still *Bob*, whatever that means, and he's still howling, but now I'm beginning to think he may have forgotten *why* he's howling, and I can't see him anymore.

Do you see what I mean about the *huh* part?

Help me.

Vincent Price says that in the original version of the movie *The Fly*, which Yvonne let me watch one night with her, but only if I promised I wouldn't get scared, and I got scared anyway.

Can things get any worse?

Yes.

They.

Certainly.

Ummm.

Can.

And then, just when it seemed to Dee Dee that things could not possibly get any worse than being in a hospital, even though her mother was sitting right by her, telling her not to be afraid and that she was brave and that everything was going to be all right, the entire hospital disappeared, and next she didn't hear anything until there was Bob the dog, introducing himself to her you-know-where.

If anyone is listening, please hurry.

35

You are right; there I stood, watching Yvonne walk away from me once again, but this time I had the feeling she would return. On the other hand, considering what she had just told me about Dee Dee's father, it *did* seem as if she had a thing for older guys. Had I known back then about Howard Bonano, I would have done something, I was pretty sure.

What a beast the man had been—but, at least, my present mandate was clear: Yvonne was a woman prone to entering into really unfortunate relationships. Ergo, I needed to perfect the Communicator, and even faster than I had thought, before she found herself enmeshed in another disaster. "You snooze, you lose," I remember someone—certainly *not* Howard Bonano—saying, and double ergo, another field test was in order, as soon as possible. That very night.

I looked outside. Some kids were throwing a baseball in the street and the guy across from me was watering his lawn, moving his hose up and down in slow arcs; it was a world of simple pleasures, for sure, but a world still too light out for me and my invention to move around without calling attention to what I was doing. It wouldn't help at all if some nervous citizen mistook me for the Park Ranger and reported me to the police. It occurred to me that in order to deflect any possible questions, it might be a good idea to make an official-looking sign that read *Monitoring in Process* and paste it on the forehead area of the helmet. That would sound just official enough to deflect any unwanted curiosity, and scary enough to cause people to keep their distance. In my experience, if you give people a reason, no matter how ridiculous, for something, they'll relax because that's the easiest thing to do. I made the sign, and it looked good. It looked so good, in fact, that I thought maybe it might be useful in some other situation as well someday, if I could only imagine one.

That still left me with a couple of hours to kill, so I turned on the television to a documentary called *Missing in Action*, which detailed what it claimed was a mysterious rise in the death rate among animals used for laboratory testing. The show asserted that what had been taken initially as an unfortunate series of accidents—cats chewing through live electric cords, dogs strangling themselves with their IV tubing—was actually more sinister than random occurrences. They were nothing less than a series of self-inflicted deaths.

Or such was the claim of the makers of the documentary. Certainly, the animals that had been in the neighboring cages of those victims were not available for interviews, themselves being mostly dead, but even if they were alive and able to speak English, in many cases their vocal cords had been removed so as not to distract the researchers with their constant complaints.

Still, the statistical evidence the program presented was disturbing, and, in addition, it showed dramatic under-cover footage of mice that had thrown themselves beneath the exercise wheels in their cages in Cleveland; it described how, in Indianapolis, six rabbits that had gone blind after weeks of shampoo being put into their eyes had nonetheless somehow hopped their way over to an adjacent area where pit bulls were kept for dentifrice testing and allowed themselves to be ripped apart. There were at least a dozen reports from all over the country of birds that had dived hard enough into the bottom of their cages to break their own necks, and even one of a swarm of fruit flies in a lab at Cornell that, having escaped its cage, had headed straight for a strip of flypaper. Sure, I thought. And why not? Why should free choice be limited to humans?

The whole situation, the voiceover said, was alarming, and not only because replacements for all these animals had to be found but also because their premature deaths created a statistical imbalance that often made a product appear dangerous for human use when it really wasn't all that bad. The program closed with a troubling question: namely, how an animal could be so selfish to take its own life when a little, or even a lot, of discomfort might one day save the life of a child. It showed a small girl in a sundress picking a flower. Then, over images of pigs and goats trying to dodge being shot and burned so that they might save the lives of our soldiers engaged in the thankless task of occupying other people's countries, the voiceover concluded, "Perhaps one day we will be able to convey the importance of sacrifice to these dumb animals, but until that day comes, they will need to continue their important work, just as brave soldiers in the human world must often do, in complete ignorance of the vital part they have played in human history."

And if those dead animals were able to communicate with us—thanks to some future development like a Communicator for pets—what would they have to say?

The program ended and at last it was dark enough to leave the house. I took a minute to change a few of the batteries in the battery pack of the Communicator, because it was frustrating not knowing how much or little juice I used on each one of my trials and whether the batteries were close to being drained. I suspected I was wasting a lot of money by changing them so often, and one of these days soon I would have to go back to Ed's and buy a decent battery charger along with a tape recorder. My to-do list was growing longer.

Finally, I was just about to pick up the helmet of the Communicator and place it over my head when I heard another knock. My first thought was that it was Yvonne returning with the money, telling me that she was sorry, but her friend couldn't accept my generosity. Or that she had made up the part about a friend.

And then, of course, it might be Dennis.

"I'm sorry to arrive so suddenly, Bob," Steadman said. "I've been talking with your next-door neighbor, Farley. I can't say I like the man very much, but he did mention that he's seen you decked out in some kind of weird headgear and carrying what he says is a flamethrower. If I'm not mistaken, he's referring to the same outfit I saw you wearing a while ago, the one you claimed was some kind of a radio receiver, or music player, or something, and the very one you have lying on your workbench right now. I'm not entirely sure I trust the man—it's my impression he's a drinker—but as a cop, I have to check out every lead, and, like it or not, he got me thinking about the other night. Now I'm not so sure that what you told me was completely the truth."

"Steadman," I said, "I can't believe you listened to that crank about anything. He's been throwing all kinds of disgusting trash into my yard for no reason at all. You see the helmet he's talking about. It's made out of egg cartons, and if it got anywhere too close to a fire, it would probably be the first thing to go. And as for the flamethrower part, I don't suppose you've heard of a directional microphone, have you? Both it and the helmet are part of a series of experiments I'm doing for the public-service sector. Can I offer you a cup of tea or anything?"

"Nice try, but not good enough, Bob," Steadman said. "Farley told me the same story about the trash, but he said you started it. And what's up with that sign that says *Monitoring in Progress*? Are you trying to pull a fast one? What happened to that classical music thing, anyway? I'd like to believe you, but when a report like this comes in, action has to be taken. Maybe we can have tea later, but for now, why don't you pick up that helmet and directional thing and we'll take them to the station? Once we get there, I'll have our own department experts take this whatever-you-call-it apparatus apart and then we'll see exactly what that thing is all about."

"OK," I said, "I admit there wasn't any *Carnival of the Animals*. This is actually a top-secret invention I'm developing, and if you can keep a secret I can tell you only that I call it the Communicator."

"Oh—and you should probably call a lawyer, too. If you don't have one, I'm sure I can persuade my sister's husband to take your case. He's not a bad guy, considering. You know this Park Ranger person isn't exactly popular down at the station, what with half the public demanding that we catch him and the other half wanting to make the guy into some kind of folk hero."

"Lawyer?" I said. "But . . ."

"Now let's get moving, Bob. You know I can do this the hard way, using the handcuffs, but I consider you a friend, so I'd appreciate it if you didn't give me any trouble."

Steadman looked tired, and I noticed for the first time that the collar of his uniform was starting to fray. He needed a woman's touch, that was for sure. *Had* he met with Yvonne since I talked to her and, if so, had she told him that she didn't want to run off with him?

I put on the vest, picked up the helmet, and grabbed the battery pack and the microphone. "Steadman," I said, "I wish you'd think this over. You're making a big mistake."

We headed outside to the squad car with me carrying the Communicator. Steadman walked behind me, just in case I made a break for it, I supposed. Beneath the light of a street lamp, I could see the dent Bob had made in the right front fender of the police cruiser.

The air was filled with the smell of burning trash and the sound of fire trucks; half of the city looked to be on fire.

"Hold it," Steadman said as we approached the car. "This time you'd better ride in back with that so-called invention of yours."

I thought I'd try one last time, with a different tack: "Steadman, have you heard anything from Yvonne recently?"

Steadman paused, as if he were deciding how to answer such a seemingly innocent question posed by a possible suspect.

And that is the way I would have liked to remember him: standing patiently next to the patrol car, weighing the possibility of private friendship versus the obligations of his public self, grappling with which should have precedence, holding the rear door open for me to enter the vehicle that I would never actually set foot inside again.

Because at that very moment I heard a rustle from the center of the bushes in front of my house, and the next thing I saw, suddenly, amazingly, and terrifyingly, was a blond-headed and flabby-but-powerful cannonball erupt from the shrubbery and strike Steadman—if he had been a ship—midhull.

Steadman rebounded from the car into which he had been shoved and fell on his back—directly, it looked like—onto his service revolver, which he kept in a holster hooked to his belt at his spine.

"Ouch," he said, and rolled over in an attempt to pull his weapon out to defend himself, but, unfortunately, the cannonball, having righted himself after his initial bull's-eye, got to it first. Dennis yanked it from Steadman's holster.

"Give me that back!"

"No, I won't!"

"Yes, you will!"

There were grunts and primitive noises, and then Dennis was waving the weapon in the air. "This is for Bob, you bastard."

Steadman started at me, uncomprehending, questioning my involvement in the matter even as he wrestled with the former Wagonmaster, attempting to retrieve his weapon.

I said nothing, but stared at the two of them as they battled, like the ghosts of a struggle I had witnessed long ago in *One Tusk*, the story of a walrus somewhere in the Arctic, in which the title character was an ancient but lovably irascible walrus who was forced to defend his harem of lady walruses against the intrusion of a much younger, two-tusked rival the program called Junior. The program had closed with the two of them rolling around on the ice, first Junior on top, and then One Tusk, as the latter punctured Junior's hide with his distinctive monosymmetrical stab marks. Would this night's battle end with the younger, more agile Dennis overcoming the man of law, or would the wily, and no doubt trained in hand-to-hand combat, Steadman regain control?

It was hard to tell.

Dennis continued to wave the gun but so far hadn't fired it.

"Bob?" Steadman looked over at me, still uncertain whether I had ordered this hit or not, but indicating that if I hadn't, it would be helpful to give him some aid in his struggle, despite the fact that he had been about to take me to the police station against my will.

"Bob, how about a hand here?"

The mention of which name incensed Dennis even more.

As I saw it, I had two choices: My first choice was to attempt to subdue the agitated Dennis and take the gun away from him—not the wisest idea, in my opinion, no matter how good a prior relationship I may have had with the man. My second choice was to don the Communicator and, as inconspicuously as possible, walk off into the dark, leaving the neighborhood behind for a little while, letting fate decide which of those two desperate individuals, each struggling with his own loss and his own deeply troubled personal history, would prevail. If, by any chance, Dennis shot Steadman, it would save Steadman a lot of future heartache vis-à-vis Yvonne, and I would be in the clear. If Steadman managed to overcome Dennis, then, by the time I returned from my walk, I would be proven innocent. It wasn't the worst spot I'd ever been in by a long shot.

Dennis took the opportunity to punch Steadman in the face several times with his free hand.

"Sorry, Steadman. Sorry, Dennis," I said. "I have miles to go before I sleep."

"What?" Steadman grunted, and he turned to grasp one of Dennis's forearms in his teeth.

I said, "And miles to go before I sleep."

I lifted the helmet of the Communicator onto my head and started walking. Along the way I passed Farley, who was rolling a wheelbarrow heaped with all manner of trash and garbage and who-knew-what-else toward my front door.

"I wouldn't go over there right now if I were you," I said, but then I realized he probably couldn't hear me through the helmet.

The light in Farley's window was on, and I could see a cat sitting there, gazing out at the dark. It was fluffy, possibly part Persian.

Meanwhile, Farley lowered his end of the wheelbarrow long enough to shake a fist at me, and his face moved silently in outraged distension. Then he lifted the handles of the wheelbarrow once again and rolled his trash-filled juggernaut in the direction of my door.

As Farley drew near, I could see that Steadman had somehow gotten the upper hand again and seemed near to regaining control of his weapon, but then Dennis rolled and was back on top, striking him again, mostly ineffectually, though it was hard to be sure in the dark. Then Steadman regained the upper hand, then Dennis, then Steadman, and so on, in a furious ball of law and disorder.

Farley stopped and stood rooted to his dull spot, trying to decide what he should do. Suddenly, yet another man arrived, this one middle-aged, on foot, and with a shock of white combed up and over his still dark and full head of hair. He was wearing a cheap suit and was holding a suitcase and a bouquet of flowers. This new individual walked up to the two combatants plus one onlooker in front of my house and stopped as well. The man looked somehow familiar, but for a moment—given the darkness and the difficulty of viewing through the slit of the Communicator, combined with the stress of the situation—I had trouble placing him.

Then it came to me. My God, I thought, it's Howard Bonano.

Howard Bonano paused, then leapt into the fray, I supposed to help anyone anywhere whom he saw engaged in combat with a representative of the law. And for a short while it looked as if he might actually turn the tide, because Howard Bonano looked to be a lot more buff, thanks to jailhouse calisthenics, than when I'd seen him last all those years ago. But apparently that was just the signal Farley was waiting for, because he jumped in as well—on Steadman's behalf—to attack Bonano. And, while the former head of the Institute for Mind/Body Research was in surprisingly good physical condition for a man his age, in its own way Farley's participation seemed to tip the scales of combat back to the uncertain middle again.

I continued down the sidewalk. I turned the corner. A light or two appeared in the bedroom windows of my neighbors, who had no doubt been awaked by the rising sounds of the desperate struggle from the street. Inside the Communicator, however, everything was as silent as a tomb.

36

Back when I was alive, I used to dream that Daddy-Shut-Your-Eyes and Mommy and I might one day all live together, like *The Little Fur Family*, but even in those days I knew it was a long shot. I mean, I wasn't stupid.

Still, I used to tell myself, "If they got together once, it could happen again."

Honestly, now I could not care less, and if I *am* some kind of ice cube, then somebody just turned up the heat.

Then time must have passed, but Dee Dee couldn't tell how much, and when she finally opened her eyes again, everything was really, really bright, like when she used to wake up in the middle of the night because she had to use the bathroom and when the light went on it almost hurt, as if Dee Dee had been slapped across her eyes and, just for a second, everything burned, but then after a second, she got used to it.

It seemed normal.

Are you still here, Bob?

37

Even with my head perfectly enclosed as it was by the vault of the Communicator's helmet, I inhaled the disturbing scent of smoke in the air, though the semifamiliar crunch of snails and dry leaves beneath my feet was comforting. But that night I sensed something had shifted in a way I could not understand. I checked my watch; it was still only about ten or ten thirty, much earlier than my previous outdoor field trial. In the future, if I wanted to speed up the perfecting of my invention, I would have to test the Communicator every hour of the day and night until I got it right. Even if Steadman was out of the way, sooner or later some other old guy would come out of the woodwork, and Yvonne would be after him like a shot. For that matter, Howard Bonano was back, too, but I figured I could count him out of the picture.

In near-perfect silence I stopped and breathed.

Someone's hibiscus was in bloom, and its sweet, musky scent mingled with the smoke like a choking, destined-to-be-supremely-unsuccessful perfume. It occurred to me to ask for the very first time, how *was* air getting inside the Communicator, anyway? If it was, might the leak, or whatever it was, be somehow spoiling the sound-deadening qualities? Yet if air wasn't getting in, then how did I keep breathing? Could the howling in my ears actually be a prelude to complete asphyxiation? Also: What would be the end result of the battle, lately turned into a tag-team match, between Steadman, Dennis, Farley, and Howard Bonano? Who would emerge as the victor?

I paused, staggered for a moment by the prospect of trying to answer so many questions that seemed to be doubling by the minute and stepped off a curb nearly straight into a fire truck as it raced in an eerie, absolute sonic vacuum toward some conflagration or another. I walked on. Through the viewing lens of the Communicator, I could see the streetlights and the occasional sweep of car headlights passing by in silence. On the legs of my pants I could feel the wet of automatic sprinklers throwing their graceful arcs like ballet dancers without an audience.

Nonetheless, there was something else about that night, besides the smoke and the relatively early hour, that seemed different, though the heavy smoke took me back to my childhood and to the smells of breakfast: burnt bacon, burnt toast, and burnt pancakes (my mother wasn't much of a cook). For a moment, I let myself be overcome in a wave of nostalgia, then raised my eyes and saw above the tops of the trees glowing plumes of fire in at least five different locations, including one that looked to be only a few blocks away. I took the helmet from my head and was surprised at how relatively quiet things were without it. There was only the faint, static sound of distant burning, but no more sirens, so either the fire truck that had nearly run me down was already on the scene, or it had passed out of earshot. On the other hand, could it be that these experiments were causing me to slowly lose my hearing? Yet another question that would have to wait for a better time to find an answer.

I returned the Communicator to my head and, as if I were a chunk of iron ore and the fire was a gigantic electromagnet—or, possibly, as if I were a ball bearing and the fire was a warped floor pulling me toward its lowest point—or, as if I were a sleepwalker stumbling forward in some secret hallucination—I found myself heading straight toward the flames.

Maybe it was a trick of the darkness, or just the odd effect of my walking in complete silence, but after a few minutes of regular motion I seemed to be no closer to the fire than when I'd begun, even though the smell of smoke had gotten stronger. My legs and feet were working correctly—I checked—and buildings passed me by as if I were in a film where the backdrop was projected on a screen while I trudged along in front of it on a treadmill—the Forgotten Man in some Hollywood Depression-era flick—but, possibly because my head was completely swaddled by the Communicator, I seemed not to be traveling at all, or rather, to be somewhere and nowhere, in a no-man's-land of time. I passed homes, apartments, vacant lots, all different and yet the same; it was a surprisingly pleasant feeling, though unusual.

Then, as if my treadmill had come suddenly over the crest of a metaphorical hill, at last I could see the actual burning building that I was being drawn to, and it was the same mysterious structure I had dreamed of the very night I had laid Bob to rest: the warehouse with the blue lower half with bars on its windows, the white second story, its windows shuttered, that place with no name that seemed so out of place, even in a dream, the building on that love seat.

I descended the metaphorical hill to find the actual fire well underway. Wherever that earlier fire-fighting equipment had been heading, it hadn't been here, that was for certain. For a moment, I wondered again what could be keeping the firemen; but when I looked out over the horizon, I saw that those earlier, small flare-ups had been joined by a gigantic conflagration in the general location of Ed's Discount Electronics. If this was the case, I could certainly understand why the St. Nils fire department had decided to concentrate its efforts there.

I took a deep breath from inside the Communicator and coughed; air was getting inside, and, at the same time, it occurred to me that in fact I had no actual information about the contents of the warehouse burning not thirty yards away from me. The place, for all I knew, might have been used as a depot to store toxic chemicals. A part of me thought that I probably should get away, and quickly, but

I couldn't; the sight of the fire held me motionless. The entire top part of the building had collapsed inwardly, onto itself, and there didn't appear to be any part of the building left unengulfed by the silent red and yellow flames. The smoke grew thicker. Around me, a few people whom I guessed were neighbors because they were dressed in bathrobes and slippers—one guy was even wearing a nightcap—had wandered up to watch. Some held hands as they cast uneasy looks in the direction of my own unusual headgear, but if they had anything to say about it, I couldn't hear them from inside my helmet. So far, at least, that monitoring sign I'd made was doing its job.

I turned the microphone off and pointed it toward the flames to let my fellow watchers know I had a purpose there, and also that I wasn't dangerous. Every so often I nodded my head, to indicate I was learning something. The truth, however, was the opposite of understanding anything at all. Somehow—and I couldn't figure out how—the Communicator was powerless to block the sounds of the fire, possibly because of the waves of energy pulsating out from the burning structure. Even with the microphone turned off, I could hear the sounds of the flames, quietly at first, but growing louder and louder, until they became a sort of painful scream so disturbing I took the helmet off and held it under my arm, at which point I was grateful to note that the sounds mysteriously diminished to the normal sounds one might expect from an ordinary burning building. There was the occasional loud pop, or crackle, or crash, but nothing near to what I had to endure with my head inside the helmet. Had the sound entered the helmet somehow, possibly under the foam neck collar, and then been trapped there? I could see a whole new page filled with more and more question marks, and I prayed Yvonne would stay in town long enough for me to answer them.

I covered my head once more with the helmet with the microphone still off, and again the sounds grew loud, then even louder—a sort of burning shriek unlike anything I could ever remember hearing. It didn't make sense.

I removed the helmet and laid it on the ground. I breathed in slowly and felt my lungs fill with smoke. For a moment, I thought the sounds I'd heard might have been caused by the duct tape on the helmet pulling away from the egg cartons as a result of being near the fire, but when I checked the wrappings, everything seemed secure. Also—and strangely—despite the intensity of the fire, the temperature outside wasn't much different than when I had first set out that night: a pleasant sixty-five or seventy degrees. The heat of whatever was burning in the warehouse must have been somehow sucked inward by means of a gigantic downdraft, if that were possible, but that same inward pulling draft left the smoke behind, contradicting everything I knew about the laws of physics, which was, admittedly, not all that much.

Why *hadn't* the fire department arrived? The sky above Ed's seemed dimmer; it looked as if that blaze might be under control. I could hear sirens in the distance, and although they seemed not to be coming closer, for one reason or another, they weren't going away either. Were they circling me, or only moving from fire to fire? I wondered if the burning building that I stood before was one of those cases where the fact of its being on fire seemed so obvious, so in need of reporting, everyone had simply assumed someone else had done it.

Then the fire's noise grew louder until it approached the level I had heard when my head was in the helmet. I looked over at those curious neighbors next to me, and they seemed frightened. Some began to quickly walk backward, away from the flames, while the rest, holding their hands over their ears, had actually begun to jog back to the comparative safety of their houses. A young though somewhat sickly looking couple was coughing deeply and holding matching green plaid scarves over their mouths as they ran. Where they had gotten the idea to bring such scarves to a fire, I had no idea, but they were smart to have done so, unlike me. My suspicion about toxic chemicals returned, and when I looked around again, I saw that I was the only one left watching the flames. It was time to go, I knew, but despite the danger, I stood there woolgathering and could not will myself to move.

I put my hands over my ears. Even with the Communicator now resting on the ground, the sounds increased to a roar like Niagara Falls as heard from that boat—whatever its name was—that takes tourists on rides to the base of the falls. I had gone there once as a child with my parents, and the experience was memorable. Then the sounds grew yet louder—a thousand times louder than before, it seemed to me.

There is a sort of paralyzing quality that a sound can produce. So much so that, according to a nature special I once watched, one of the reasons polar bears, lions, and tigers roar is to render their prey immobile. Thus, there I stood in the face of that roaring fire, overwhelmed and unable to move, even though at that moment I wanted nothing more than to turn, to retreat, to flee, to head for home, as all those sensible neighbors had done. But no. There I stayed, alone in the burning night, the Communicator lying at my feet beside me like a second, larger, and even more useless head, my hands crushing my ears in an effort to dim the sound, the expression on my face—though I could not see it—a grotesque mask of pain and questioning.

I shut my eyes, as if that would somehow help.

It did not.

I opened them again.

I removed a hand from one of my ears to check my watch. Its dial, lit by the flames, showed it was nearly midnight. Where had the time gone? But even more baffling, at the moment I took my hand away from my head, the level of sound that entered my unprotected ear was exactly the same as the sound that entered the covered one. I put my hand back over my ear and took it away one more time. It was true. The sound that filled my ears was not just the sound of a single warehouse caught on fire in a small nocturnal town—something, if you think about it, that's not so unusual—but had in some exponential manner multiplied into the sound of the entire earth: my town, my state, my people, my species, the clamor of every living thing as well as all the dead, the entire planet burning up all at once, as if the fire were no longer simply flames, but had been transformed into liquid, and some fool had opened the floodgates deep inside the universe, so that what used to be flames and heat and light was now streaming in one gigantic liquid, sonic, and fiery tsunami, the sound of everything from the beginning of time until that moment, condensed into one endless, single noise that was impossible to break down into separate parts: no sentences, no words, not even any language I could recognize—and certainly not English—but all languages and all sounds ever made, both animal and human. And still I stood there on that fiery shore, rooted to the pavement, struck dumb and unable to move even an inch, the Communicator resting at my feet like a faithful pet.

I listened and, despite having heard enough, I remained. I gave a shout and the sound of my shout disappeared without a trace into the larger sound around me as if it were no more than silence.

As the walls of the warehouse collapsed all at once, I sank to my knees next to that useless waste of time, the Communicator, and I then kept on watching until at last I could see with my own eyes, even smarting as they were from smoke coming out of the almost completely gutted structure, silhouetted against a backdrop of flames by then pure white—though *still* without any discernible heat—what appeared to be the shapes of a young girl and a fair-sized dog together, who although I couldn't exactly tell what condition either of them were in, didn't look too good, but were nonetheless walking slowly toward me.

Once again I would like to thank my amazing Tin House editors, Lee Montgomery and Meg Storey, for their insight and patience, also Luke Gerwe, whose excellent proofreading extended well beyond the call of duty. And even before they saw the manuscript, I'm grateful to Janice Shapiro and Monona Wali for steering me away from some of my more disastrous impulses.

ELKINS PARK FREE LIBRARY
563 CHURCH ROAD
ELKINS PARK, PA 19027-2445